Rush

HANDS AROUND LINCOLN SCHOOL

FRANK ASCH

AN
APPLE
PAPERBACK

D0060557

SCHOLASTIC INC.
New York Toronto London Auckland Sydney

To
Hilary, Kate,
Angela, and Chalon

Contents

1.
Winds of Doom

"I can't talk now," said Lindsay. "Just come over quick. It's an emergency!"

I didn't stop to think. I just grabbed my coat and scrambled downstairs.

Crunch! As I launched myself past my little brother's room, I felt something snap beneath my heel.

"Mommy!" screamed Derrick, "Amy crushed Captain Bones!"

Captain Bones is my little brother's favorite toy soldier.

"Sorry, Derrick," I called over my shoulder.

"No you're not!" hollered Derrick. "But you're gonna be sorry, *real* sorry!"

Under normal conditions, Derrick's threat would send shivers down my spine, but I couldn't think about him now. I kept hearing the utter terror in Lindsay's voice as she said, "It's an emergency!" Had some kind of accident occurred? A fire, perhaps? Or had the kitchen stove exploded? When I turned the corner onto her street, would I see the contents of Lindsay's house and her mother in a pool of blood lying on the sidewalk?

I knew Lindsay's mom had been under a lot of strain lately. Had the pressure of earning a living and being a single mom finally pushed her over the edge? Or had Lindsay's father returned? Lindsay told me about the arguments her parents had before the divorce. I quickened my pace as I imagined them throwing frying pans at one another.

Then I recalled Lindsay telling me something about a doctor's appointment. Had they found a lump? A brain tumor? If only Lindsay had taken the time to tell me what was wrong. Without a clue to go on, the suspense of not knowing was driving me crazy.

Lindsay's house isn't far from mine. Just a five-minute walk if you stick to the streets. But I took the shortcut through Mr. Larson's backyard. Mr. Larson is one of the grumpiest people in Westfield. He thinks nothing of calling the cops if anyone so much as breathes on his property. But that didn't seem to matter now. All I could do was think of Lindsay, and hope she was still alive by the time I arrived!

Yesterday's snow had drifted during the night and slowed me down, but I made it to Lindsay's in record time. Gasping for breath, I rang the bell and waited. There were no strange cars parked out front or in the driveway. "I guess that's a good sign," I said to myself. Finally Lindsay, her eyes all red from crying, answered the door.

"Oh, Lindsay, I came as soon as I could. What is it? What's wrong?" I grabbed Lindsay's hand and waited for some response.

Lindsay attempted to smile, but it came off looking more like a grimace.

I could see Mrs. Morgan out of the corner of my eye. She was *not* trading punches with her ex-husband. She was in the den working at her word processor.

"Come into my room," said Lindsay. "We can talk there."

Lindsay sat down in the middle of her bed, and I eased into the comfortable beanbag chair by the window.

The smell of cedar shavings filled the room. For a while, we sat in silence. Besides the clicking of Carol's word processor (Lindsay calls her mom by her first name), the only sound that could be heard was the squeak of Marvin's exercise wheel. Marvin is Lindsay's pet mouse.

Twice Lindsay tried to speak, but nothing came out.

"Come on, Linds. Are you sick? Did someone die? Remember our pledge. You *have* to tell me."

Lindsay knew what I was talking about. Years ago we swore on a Bible to tell each other *all* our problems, even the big ones that we couldn't tell anyone else.

"It's just so tragic," sighed Lindsay. "The poor animals didn't have a chance!"

Suddenly I realized that Lindsay's two cats, Tinker and Bell, were not in the room. Tinker and Bell were like dogs. They rarely left Lindsay's side.

"Oh, that's so terrible!" I said, picturing the two cats torn to pieces by the neighbor's Doberman. "How did it happen?"

"Pollution, riots, famine, and then, nuclear war!" replied Lindsay.

Nuclear war?

Just then Tinker and Bell pushed open Lindsay's door and hopped on to her bed.

"Lindsay, what poor animals are you talking about?"

"The ones I just saw on TV. Oh, Amy, it wasn't just animals. The whole planet was destroyed!"

"Lindsay Morgan" — I stood up and looked her straight in the eye — "Do you mean to tell me that you called me all the way over here on a perfectly good Saturday afternoon because of something you saw on television?"

"I tried to call sooner so you could watch it, too, but I just couldn't tear my eyes from the screen. Then your line was busy."

"You said it was an emergency!" I snapped. "I didn't know what to think!"

"I'm sorry," said Lindsay, "I really am. But Carol's

4

got a deadline. I had no one to talk to."

"An emergency, for your information, is like when your house is on fire or somebody is strangling you, which I feel like doing right now!" I told her.

"I just had to talk to someone," said Lindsay, snatching up her pillow and clutching it to her chest.

Lindsay looked so down, I couldn't stay angry with her for long.

"What was this program?" I asked, noticing a soothing tone creeping into my voice almost against my own will. "Some kind of documentary?"

"It was a science fiction movie called *Winds of Doom*," replied Lindsay. "But it's not what you think. It wasn't about giant spiders, robot aliens, or anything corny like that. It started with Earth's pollution problems getting worse and worse. Then people couldn't go outside anymore because the ozone layer was totally destroyed. There were giant oil spills, famines, and, finally, a nuclear war. In the end there were just a handful of people living in caves, eating insects, and drinking radioactive slime."

"Fun movie," I said.

"It was the scariest movie I ever saw," said Lindsay, "and the plot was based on real facts. Did you know that 24 million people die of starvation every year? Ninety acres of rain forests are being destroyed every minute, and the world spends $2 billion on armaments every *day!*"

"Did you know you scared me half to death?" I replied.

"Look, I said I was sorry!" Lindsay apologized again. "But don't you see, Amy? We've been living in a dreamworld. All those nights sitting up late in our pajamas, eating popcorn, and talking about what it's going to be like in the future when we grow up. Well, if people don't wake up soon, there isn't going to be a future!"

"Oh, come on, Lindsay," I said, stroking Tinker, who was now curled up in my lap. "It was just a movie."

Bell, getting jealous, nudged my foot, so I picked her up, too.

"But, Amy, it could happen. Even if we don't incinerate ourselves with H-bombs, we're slowly but surely choking ourselves to death in our own garbage and pollution."

"So what's new?" I said. "We've been hearing grown-ups talk about that kind of stuff since we were little kids."

"Sure they talk about it," said Lindsay, "but every day things just get worse and worse, and what are they *doing* about it? What are *we* doing about it?"

"Not much," I replied, "but isn't that why we elect people to Congress and send presidents to the White House?"

"Saving the earth is too important a task to leave to congress people and presidents!" said Lindsay, flinging her pillow to the floor. "If ordinary people like you and me don't step into the fight, our Mother Earth may not survive the twenty-first century!"

"Sure, Linds, two sixth-grade girls are going to save the world!"

Suddenly Lindsay sat bolt upright. "Oh, Amy! I've just had a *great* idea! I *knew* talking to you would get my creative juices going!"

Lindsay has been having *great ideas* ever since I've known her. When we were four years old, she convinced me that we could eat mud pies if we baked them in her mother's oven. A few years later one of her great ideas was to take two little boys with us to church and ask the local priest to marry us. Then there was the great idea Lindsay had in second grade to save all the stray cats and dogs in town by putting them in *my* cellar.

"Oh, no! Not another great idea!" I groaned. "Please, Lindsay, anything but that!"

"Relax, Amy. It's simple. . . ."

Most of Lindsay's great ideas begin with the phrase, "It's simple. . . ." Unfortunately, they rarely end that way.

"Your idea of simple is going over Niagara Falls *without* a barrel," I said. "Why don't we just save ourselves a lot of trouble and go Christmas shopping or something?"

But Lindsay was not in the mood to go shopping.

"This year, as the upperclass persons of Lincoln School," she said with a big smile that rapidly blossomed into a beaming grin, "I propose that we set a good example for all the lower grades by starting our own Save the Earth Club."

"A what?" I said.

"A Save the Earth Club," said Lindsay. "It wouldn't have to be big to start with, just you, me, and the twins. Now isn't that a *great* idea?"

2.
The Twins

Before I could say anything, Lindsay picked up the phone and called Ruth and Heather's house.

"No answer," she said. "But you know the twins. They're probably playing their radio so loud, no one can hear the phone ring."

"Or they're out Christmas shopping," I ventured, lowering Tinker to the floor.

There have been times when I've managed to steer clear of one of Lindsay's great ideas. Like the summer she decided to have a séance in her backyard for kids who wanted to contact the spirits of their dead pets. But I had to admit this particular great idea intrigued me.

"What's this Save the Earth Club actually going to do?" I asked.

"Lots of things," said Lindsay. "Trust me. It's going to be *dynamic*!"

"Dynamic" is Lindsay's newest favorite word. Before

dynamic she was into *massive*. And before that, everything was either *brilliant* or *intense*.

"Going out!" Lindsay called to her mother and swung open the front door.

Whooosh! A blast of cold air made me wish I had taken the time to grab my gloves from the hall table.

"I trusted you with Dial-a-Giggle," I said as we strode down the sidewalk leaping over occasional piles of snow.

Dial-a-Giggle was another one of Lindsay's great ideas. It was supposed to make us millionaires, but ended up costing us $9.45 each. I'll spare you the gory details.

"Oh! You can't compare this idea to Dial-a-Giggle," said Lindsay. "That was just a get-rich-quick scheme. This idea has the mark of *destiny*. It will be our contribution to humanity. Something we can look back on when we're grandmothers and say to our grandchildren, 'Yes, we helped save the earth!' "

"Mark of destiny," I moaned. "Give me a break."

I hadn't noticed how cold it was on the way to Lindsay's, but now it seemed like the wind was trying to attack me, creeping under my collar and through the zipper of my coat.

"Doesn't the fate of Mother Earth mean *anything* to you?" asked Lindsay.

"Sure it does," I replied, "but there's just so much time in a school day. And, well, to tell you the truth,

10

I was thinking about joining the drama club this semester."

"The drama club!" Lindsay rolled her eyeballs in obvious disapproval. Lindsay isn't anti-drama or anything like that. She just doesn't like a certain group of sixth graders that more or less dominate the drama club. I don't particularly like them, either. They may be the best-looking, smartest, most popular kids at Lincoln School, but boy do they know it! Lindsay and I call them the "cool clique."

"I just thought being in the drama club might help me with my problem," I explained.

My problem is shyness. Not around my friends, of course. But when it comes to meeting new people, especially boys, or getting up in front of a group, I just get really scared. For some time now, Lindsay has taken it upon herself to help me with my problem. She's always encouraging me to talk louder, and throw back my shoulders. Last year she convinced me that I ought to change my wardrobe. "Bright colors, baggy T-shirts, and sneakers instead of skirts and sweaters," she said. "That'll do it." She even had me talking to myself in front of a mirror with marbles in my mouth!

"Believe me, becoming a member of the cool clique isn't going to help your problem!" said Lindsay.

"I said I was thinking of joining the drama club, *not* the cool clique!" I told her in no uncertain terms.

Lindsay thought for a moment. "Well, maybe it

would be good for you to join the drama club, but why not join the Save the Earth Club, too?"

"You want the straight, honest-to-god truth?" I said.

"Don't I always?" said Lindsay.

"All right, then," I said. "In a word, the answer is *grades*. Not everyone is a whiz like you."

Lindsay winced at that. She doesn't like being called a "whiz," but it's true. She always gets straight A's unless she gets some teacher mad at her.

"I thought your report card last semester was the best ever," said Lindsay.

"It was," I replied. "But apparently it only whetted my parents' appetite. The first day I brought it home, they said, 'We're so proud of you.' The second day they said, 'We knew you could do it,' and by the third day, they were saying, 'Next time you'll do much better,' which was the exact same thing they said when I brought home a lousy report card."

"So why bother with grades?" said Lindsay.

"Because I want to get into a good college."

"You mean because your parents want you to get into a good college," said Lindsay.

"Same difference," I replied. "They won't be happy until I'm elected first woman president of the United States."

"But don't you see?" said Lindsay. "That's precisely why we're having a Save the Earth Club."

"So I can be president when I grow up?"

"So there can be a United States when you grow up," said Lindsay.

When we arrived at the twins' house, we met their dad stringing Christmas lights on a pathetic-looking cedar tree in the front yard. This scrawny evergreen was so weighted down with decorations, it looked like it might snap in two.

"Ruth and Heather are upstairs," said Mr. Costello, adding yet another string of lights to the tree. "They've got their CD player on, so don't bother knocking. Just go on in."

We had already taken a few steps toward the house when Lindsay stopped and called back to Mr. Costello, "I hope you don't leave those lights on all night long, Mr. Costello."

Mr. Costello just smiled. "I wouldn't think of it."

"Good," said Lindsay. "Every time we save electricity, we're helping to save the planet."

"You say you want a rev-o-lu-tion. Well, you know . . . we'd all like to see the plan." John Lennon's voice throbbed through the twins' bedroom door.

I knocked, but there was no response.

"You've got to knock louder than that," said Lindsay and she pounded on the door with both fists.

"Hey, be cool," hollered Ruth, opening the door just a crack. "Far out!" she squealed. "We were just going to call you guys."

"Are you gonna let us in or what?" said Lindsay.

"Not yet." Ruth pulled her head in and shut the door.

"Hey, what's the big idea?" called Lindsay, shouting to be heard over the music.

"And if you go carrying pictures of Chairman Mao . . . you ain't gonna make it with anyone anyhow. . . ."

"You'll see," cried Heather from behind the door. "Gosh these jeans are tight!"

A minute or so went by.

Lindsay and I just looked at one another and listened to the music.

"But when you talk about destruction, you know that you can count me out . . ."

"How long are you going to keep us out here?" called Lindsay.

"Okay, we're ready," echoed Heather. "You can come in now!"

As we opened the door, we saw Ruth and Heather standing on their beds dressed in authentic sixties hippie garb: bell-bottoms, tie-dyed T-shirts, headbands, and endless strands of wooden beads.

"Well, how do we look?" asked Heather.

"Groovy," said Lindsay.

In case you didn't know, "groovy" is an old sixties word. It means *neat* or *cool.*

Ruth turned around with her arms stretched out like a fashion model. "You really like it?" she asked.

14

"You both look absolutely dynamic!" exclaimed Lindsay.

With their long blonde hair, slim bodies, and delicate features, the twins could wear old tire tubes and leftover spaghetti and still look terrific.

Next to the twins, I think Lindsay and I come off looking kind of drab. Lindsay is thin and has very beautiful curly black hair. But she's the shortest sixth grader at Lincoln School. As for me, well, I'm very *too*. My face is too round. My mouth is too small. My brown hair is too straight and I've got too many freckles.

"Where did you get those bell-bottoms?" I asked Ruth.

Lindsay and I have been searching everywhere for bell-bottoms.

"We made them ourselves," said Ruth. "We just opened up a seam and added an extra panel."

"So it didn't cost much?" I said.

"Not a penny," said Heather.

The twins have been into sixties stuff ever since they were little and dressed their Barbie and Ken dolls in hippie clothes. They called Barbie "Tanya," and Ken, "Road." They even made Barbie and Ken a hippie van out of a toy truck and painted flowers and peace signs on it with nail polish. "Tanya" and "Road" were always going to Woodstock and getting their hippie van stuck in the mud. Lindsay and I are into sixties

15

stuff, too, but not as much as Ruth and Heather. That would be impossible.

"Come on, Heather," said Ruth, jumping off her bed. "Let's show them our peace handshake!"

"Okay," giggled Heather, stepping down.

Grinning at one another, the twins held out their right hands with two fingers extended to form the traditional V-shaped peace sign.

"Wait a minute, this is serious," said Heather and she forced herself to wipe the sheepish grin off her face. Ruth did the same. "Okay, now we're ready."

The two girls interlocked their extended fingers and shook their hands up and down.

"That's it?" said Lindsay.

"That's it," said Heather. "Want to try?"

"Sure," said Lindsay and she did the peace handshake, first with Heather, and then Ruth.

"Far out!" she cried. "For a moment it was like I had slipped back in time to the sixties."

"Maybe you did!" said Ruth in a spooky voice, and we all laughed.

That's what it's like hanging out with the twins. We always laugh a lot.

Finally Lindsay told the twins her great idea.

"It would be like having Earth Day at Lincoln School all year long," was the way she explained it.

The twins thought Lindsay's Save the Earth Club

was the greatest idea since the invention of blue jeans.

"Very hip! I love it!" squealed Ruth.

"Psychedelic!" swooned Heather. "But Christmas vacation isn't over for ten whole days! There must be something we can do in the meantime."

"Wait a minute! I saw something interesting in yesterday's junk mail," said Ruth and she ran out of the room.

"That letter about saving whales?" Heather called after her.

"That's the one," replied Ruth.

"I saw it, too," said Heather. "Look on Dad's desk."

In less than a minute, Ruth reappeared with an envelope in her hand. "Here it is," she said, taking a piece of paper from the envelope. "It's amazing how well organized our parents are. They have a place for everything, even junk mail."

"Can I see that?" Lindsay snatched the paper and began to read. "Mmmm, this sounds dynamic!" she mused. "Only fifteen bucks to adopt a whale."

"Adopt a whale? Even a baby whale is enormous. Where would we keep it?" I said, thinking out loud. "Not in my cellar!"

"Really, Amy! Sometimes you're so naive," snickered Lindsay. "Adopting a whale is not like adopting a baby. You don't get to keep it. You send in your money, and they use it to study and protect whales."

"They send you photos, and you pick a whale," said Ruth. "Every so often they send you reports about how your whale is doing."

"Groovyolla!" exclaimed Heather. "Let's do it!"

"Well, how about it, Amy?" Lindsay turned to me. "You with us?"

I still had my doubts. For openers, the connection between spending fifteen dollars on adopting a whale that we were never actually going to see and saving the world from pollution, famine, and nuclear war was not as clear in my mind as it apparently ought to be. But let's face it. Lindsay, Ruth, and Heather are my best friends. Even if they had a "Let's All Go to School Wrapped in Toilet Paper Club," I probably would have joined.

"Okay!" I said. "I'm with you."

"Extra-dimensional groovy!" cried Ruth, and we all did the peace handshake.

3.
Nuts and Bolts

"Okay, step one," said Lindsay. "Give me a pad and paper and I'll write down how much money we've got. Then I'll subtract that from fifteen dollars, and we'll know how much money we need to raise to adopt a whale."

Lindsay's a dreamer all right, but when it comes to getting things done, she's all nuts and bolts. A real doer. The same, however, could not be said of the twins.

"Pad and paper!" they exclaimed, stumbling over one another as they scrambled around the room.

"Scissors, stickers, thread, paste," Ruth called out the names of various objects as she rummaged through the layers of debris on top of her desk. Then Heather opened her closet, and an avalanche of junk tumbled out onto her sandals.

"Hey, look, here's Pumpkin!" said Ruth, holding up a plastic lizard painted in disgusting shades of Day-

Glo orange and green. "I've been looking all over for you."

"Sorry," said Heather, "I can't find any paper or a pen right now. Maybe I ought to start looking for something else."

"Why would you do that?" I asked.

"It's my new method for finding things," said Heather. "It's based on the fact that I always find what I *was* looking for when I'm looking for something else."

"I found a red crayon!" cried Ruth.

"Never mind," replied Lindsay, spying a pocket calculator sticking out of one of Ruth's pink rabbit slippers. "This will do."

"Okay," said Lindsay, "I'm flat broke." She entered a zero on the calculator.

"Us, too," said Heather. "We spent our last dime on beads."

Lindsay entered two more zeros. "This doesn't look good," she said. Suddenly, all eyes were on me.

"Hey, don't look at me," I said.

"Come on," said Lindsay. "Everyone knows what a terrific little penny-pincher you are."

I resent the term "penny-pincher." Sure, I'm careful with my money. But I hate it when people accuse me of "squeaking," and "being tight." Just because I'm not as wasteful as they are doesn't automatically make me a *tightwad*.

"It's Christmastime, remember?" I said. "I just

bought my mom a bottle of Chanel No. 5."

"Don't you have anything left over in that piggy bank of yours?" said Lindsay in an accusing tone of voice.

Lindsay was referring to the pink ceramic pig that I've kept next to my bed since I was seven years old. Chipped now from years of wear, it has a big slot on top but no hole on the bottom. It's easy to put money in, hard to shake it out. I call it Piggy.

"I have a few dollars," I said, "but I'm going to have to spend most of that to buy Derrick a new Captain Bones for Christmas."

"You're going to buy Derrick a war toy for Christmas?" said Lindsay. "That's the last thing that little storm trooper needs!"

"Oh, leave Amy alone," said Ruth. "Even if she chipped in all the money from Piggy, we'd still need to come up with more cash to adopt a whale."

"Okay," sighed Lindsay. "Let's see. Fifteen minus zero minus zero minus zero minus zero equals fifteen!" She stuffed the calculator back into Ruth's bunny slipper. "Now at least we know how much money we need to raise: fifteen dollars!"

So far, we were progressing along the well-worn path established by Lindsay's other great ideas: nowhere fast.

"Maybe we could go to town and panhandle," said Ruth.

21

"What if our parents walked by?" said Heather. "That wouldn't be cool."

"We could wear disguises!" said Ruth. "I'll wear a gray wig and be an old bag lady. I've always wondered what it's like to wander the streets muttering to myself."

Ruth and Heather still love to play dress-up. They maintain a giant collection of dress-up clothes in their closet. In fact, one of their favorite games is turning their bedroom into a boutique. "Boutique Unique," they call it. They even cut out pictures from magazines and made a Boutique Unique catalog.

"Yeah, and I'll get a cane and an eyepatch," said Heather, "and maybe we can sing songs and make chalk drawings on the sidewalk and . . ."

"Come on, you guys, get serious," said Lindsay.

The twins looked at Lindsay with dismay. As far as they were concerned, they *were* being serious.

"We can't just go around pretending to be old and destitute," said Lindsay. "It's not right."

"But we are destitute," said Ruth, "aren't we?"

"Not like the homeless people who *have* to be out on the streets," said Lindsay.

"Lindsay's right," said Heather. "It would be like making fun of homeless people."

"What a bummer," groaned Ruth. "This *is* a problem."

"Don't worry," I told her. "It's only a matter of time

before Lindsay comes up with some half-baked great idea."

"Zingo! That's it!" Lindsay jumped to her feet. "I just had *another* dynamic idea! And it's not half-baked. It's completely baked!"

"Don't tell me. Let me guess," I said. "We're going to peddle stocks in a phony gold mine. No, better yet, we're going to sell ourselves into the white slave trade? Am I close?"

"Wrong, Miss Wisecrack," said Lindsay. Then she paused for dramatic effect before announcing with a self-assured flourish, "We're going to have . . . a bake sale!"

"OOOOh! I like it!" crooned Ruth.

"Right on!" echoed Heather. "Lindsay, you're a genius!"

"I bet Shoppers' Choice would let us have one in their store," said Lindsay. "They always have lots of fund-raising events, especially around Christmastime."

"Our dad knows a man who works in the produce department," said Ruth. "I bet he could help us get permission."

"I knew this would work!" exclaimed Lindsay. "A few hours ago I was feeling all gloom and doom! Now things are looking brighter already. Today we save a whale. Tomorrow the planet!"

4.
The Avenger

For the rest of the afternoon we hung out at Ruth and Heather's house, ate stale potato chips, and talked about our Save the Whales Bake Sale.

When I got home, I found a note on my desk:

You crushed his head,
Now Captain Bones is dead,
His pain is done,
But yours has just begun.
Signed
The Avenger

Of course I knew right away who wrote the note. He might as well have signed it with his own name.

Derrick has soft, light brown hair and a sweet, angel-like face, but he's not the kind of kid you'd want to have for an enemy. When it comes to revenge, Derrick

24

is in a gifted category. No matter what the offense, he always gets even, and then some.

One day I made the mistake of teasing Derrick about having a crush on his second-grade teacher. At the time, he didn't react at all. But two weeks later, he went out of his way to get me in big trouble with Mom and Dad.

"See what happens to girl creeps who tease their little brothers?" he gloated.

"Squealer!" I hollered.

"It wasn't me," he protested. "I'm no squealer. It must have been The Avenger!"

Since then, whenever I step out of line, Derrick takes his Avenger idea out of mothballs. One time at the beach I used Derrick's towel without asking. Three days later, coming out of the house I was struck on the head by a giant water balloon. In the balloon was a soggy note:

This time use your own towel!
The Avenger

If Derrick ever writes a book, he could call it *Creative Revenge*, or, *How to Drive Your Sister Absolutely Bonkers.*

Captain Bones is not only Derrick's favorite toy soldier, it was the first one he ever owned. As far as

Derrick is concerned, Captain Bones is the smartest, strongest, bravest toy soldier that ever existed. So The Avenger was not likely to show me any mercy. Any door I opened could be booby-trapped. My alarm clock could be wired to give an electric shock. Any morning I could wake up and find glue in my shoes.

It took me almost a half hour to shake enough coins out of Piggy to buy Derrick a new Captain Bones. I just hoped it would make The Avenger go easy on me. After all, I did say I was sorry. And what's more, I meant it. That had to count for something.

That night after dinner, Lindsay called. "Good news," she said. "Ruth and Heather's father talked to his friend at Shoppers' Choice. Everything is set for next Saturday."

"That didn't take long," I said.

"If we're going to save the earth, we have to work fast," said Lindsay. "Can you have five dozen brownies baked by then?"

"Sure," I said, "but don't you think that's an awful lot of brownies to sell in one day?"

"Don't worry about that," said Lindsay. "I'm sure we'll figure out what to do with the leftovers." Meaning eat them, of course.

"What did you decide on? The whale-shaped cookies, or the cupcakes with the peace signs on top?" I asked.

"The cupcakes," said Lindsay, "and I'm not going

26

to eat a single one of them until after the bake sale is over."

"Don't tell me you're on a diet," I said.

No one would call Lindsay overweight, but every once in a while she goes on a diet eating nothing but carrot sticks and celery. It's so absurd. All it ever does is make her irritable and obsessed with food. But this time it wasn't a diet.

"No diet," she said. "I just don't want to eat up all the profits. Once I start tasting, things get out of hand and into mouth. If you know what I mean?"

"Yeah, one nibble and it's all over for me, too," I said. "I taste one brownie and the next thing I know, I'm staring at a half-empty plate."

"Let's pledge not to taste a single cupcake or brownie," said Lindsay.

"Done!" I said.

"Done!" echoed Lindsay.

I'm not much of a cook. Whenever I fry eggs, for example, they come out either runny or looking like I tried to incinerate them in a pottery kiln. I can just look at a stove and give people indigestion. But I *can* bake brownies. In fact, I think I can say with all due modesty that I'm the best little brownie baker this side of Ms. Lehmer's 4-H club. My brownies always come out rich and moist. Not too sweet, not too chewy, not too dry, but j-u-s-t right.

By Friday night I had baked six dozen brownies, one dozen more than Lindsay had asked for. I was quite proud of the fact that I hadn't tasted a single one of them. I was also proud of the fact that I had succeeded in protecting them from Derrick's all-consuming mouth.

The night before the bake sale, Lindsay called to make sure everything was okay.

"Don't forget to take your brownies out of the freezer tonight," she said.

"Don't worry, I took care of it already. Who's bringing the money box?"

"I am," said Lindsay.

I was sitting at the kitchen counter before a huge pile of nearly thawed brownies. Somehow, my anxiety about tomorrow was causing my hand to reach out and grab for one.

"You aren't gobbling up any of the profits are you?" asked Lindsay.

"Who me?" I said.

At that very moment, as if guided by remote control, my arm was aiming a brownie toward my mouth.

"Just remember," said Lindsay, "every brownie you eat is one less for the whales."

By a sheer act of will I forced my hand into reverse, put the brownie back, and replaced the waxed paper.

"Well, I hope you're not eating any of the whales' cupcakes," I said. "You know how they *love* cupcakes."

28

5.
Save the Whales Bake Sale

Any other Saturday morning, dynamite couldn't have gotten me out of bed earlier than ten o'clock. But the Saturday of our Save the Whales Bake Sale I was dressed and ready to go at eight-thirty. By nine o'clock I was standing in front of the Shoppers' Choice with the twins waiting in the shivering cold for someone to open the door and let us in.

"Where's Lindsay?" I asked, sending my wispy white breath toward the blinking red neon sign above our heads.

"I thought she was coming with you," replied Ruth, stomping her feet to keep warm.

"You know Lindsay," said Heather. "She probably stopped at the library."

Lindsay is a *voracious* reader. Voracious is the word my mother uses to describe Derrick's appetite. The first time I heard it I thought it meant violent. But even Derrick doesn't have a violent appetite. Anyway, Lindsay loves to read books. You could deliver a dump truck load of books to her door once a week and she'd still complain about not having enough to read.

Finally a lumpy-looking man with slicked-down hair and wire-rimmed glasses opened the door and let us in.

"I'm the manager, Mr. Stillwell," he said, hardly looking up from the clipboard that he held in his hand. "You can set up your table by the bottle return. Just don't block traffic, and remember you have to be out of here by one-thirty. That's when the Boy Scouts will be coming in to sell candy."

"He's not very friendly," whispered Heather as we carried in our stuff.

"I think he's seen one too many bake sales," said Ruth.

While I unpacked my brownies, the twins spread a red-and-white-checkered tablecloth over the card table they brought to display our wares.

Then Ruth taped her poster to the window behind our table. It was a picture of Earth as seen from space done in watercolors with a caption that read, "LOVE YOUR MOTHER."

Both Ruth and Heather are talented artists. But Ruth's paintings are special. I wouldn't be surprised if she became a real artist some day.

"It's not original," said Ruth. "I saw it on a T-shirt."

"But, Ruth," I gushed, "it's just so beautiful."

"Anyone could have done it," she said.

Anyone but me, I thought to myself. I'm all thumbs when it comes to art. The only thing I can draw is stick figures, and they always end up looking more like piles of pick-up sticks than people.

Even before we had everything set up, potential customers were starting to look over our goods. Our first paying customer was a tiny, gray-haired woman who remembered me from two years ago.

"Are you the youngster who used to bake brownies for the 4-H club?" she asked, tilting her head to see first me and then the brownies on the table through her bifocals.

"That's me," I answered.

"Well, I've tasted many a batch of brownies in my time," she informed me, "but I don't mind saying yours were the best brownies I ever had!"

"Ah . . . er . . ." Suddenly my voice dropped to a whisper like it always does when I'm embarrassed. Luckily, Ruth, sensing my predicament, started talking to the old lady.

"We're using all the money we make to help whales," she said.

"That's very nice of you," replied the old lady. "We need a lot more *jails* nowadays. A woman my age just isn't safe on the street anymore."

"No, it's not *jails* we're trying to help," said Heather, "it's *whales*."

"Oh, whales!" said the old lady. "They're nice, too."

Ruth handed the old lady her change. But she refused to take it. "You can keep that for the whales," she said.

Judging from the old cloth coat she was wearing, I took her act of generosity as something more than just a showy gesture.

Ruth put the money in her pocket, and the old woman eased her shopping cart toward the frozen food department. As I watched her go, I wished that I hadn't had a shyness attack. It would have been nice to chat with her.

"Where's Lindsay?" I wondered out loud. "We need that money box. Not everyone is going to let us keep the change!" I noticed how angry my voice sounded. That's how it is with me. First I get shy, then I get annoyed.

I used to be incredibly shy. Even little things could send me into my shell. One time, in third grade, when the teacher called roll at the beginning of class, I was so shy, I couldn't answer "here," and she marked me absent.

"Here comes Lindsay now," said Heather.

Lindsay, wearing a bright pink and electric-blue ski jacket, was carrying a large cardboard box. Lindsay likes to wear bright colors. Her favorite is hot pink.

"Sorry I'm late, but I stopped at the library to get us some reading material." Lindsay plopped the cardboard box on the floor next to our table. "How are we doing?"

"Not bad," said Heather. "We made four dollars already."

"Dynamic!" exclaimed Lindsay.

"Did you bring the money box?" I asked.

"Right here." Lindsay opened the flaps of the cardboard carton and took out her father's fishing tackle box. "I remember this tackle box from when my dad used to take me fishing," she sighed.

Lindsay doesn't talk about it much, but I know she misses her father a lot. Her parents have been divorced for over a year. In the beginning, it wasn't so bad. Lindsay used to visit her father every other weekend. But recently he moved to California. Now all she gets are telephone calls and letters.

Lindsay reached down into the cardboard carton and lifted out two plates of cupcakes.

"Smells great!" said Ruth. "And I love the peace signs you made on top. The colors are really groovy."

"Someday I'm going to be a baking artist," said Lindsay.

"Baking artist?" asked Heather.

"Yeah," said Lindsay, "I'll bake beautiful pictures in dough and use dried fruit and other stuff for colors. Like cherries for red, licorice for black, and chocolate chips for brown."

33

"Your paintings wouldn't last long," said Heather.

"That's the whole point," grinned Lindsay. "Instead of hanging on the wall in some stupid museum to collect dust, people will eat them."

"Then what?" I asked.

"Then I'd bake some more art," chuckled Lindsay. "Let them eat art! That's my motto."

Actually, Lindsay's an even worse artist than I am. My stick figures may not look human, but her stick figures don't even look like sticks. But does that stop Lindsay from thinking about being an artist someday? No way!

The rest of Lindsay's cardboard box contained almost a dozen books.

I checked out some of the titles. *Pollution and You, Garbage and You, Saving the Rain Forest, Save the Animals, 101 Easy Things You Can Do to Save the Earth.* I looked through them all and picked out a book called *Sadako and the Thousand Paper Cranes.*

"Can I borrow this one?" I asked.

"Oh, that one's dynamic," said Lindsay. "Sure, you can borrow it. That's why I got them. I figured if we're going to raise consciousness at Lincoln School, we ought to have a little of it ourselves. On the way here I was reading some interesting facts."

Lindsay's such a compulsive reader, she even reads while she walks.

"Take this store, for example. It's a prime example

of ecological waste. Did you know that most Americans throw out their own weight in packaging every thirty to forty days? And by the age of seventy-five, a child born in the United States will have produced fifty-two tons of garbage and use five times more energy than a child born in a third-world country. Isn't that gross?"

"Not as gross as the stuff on this table," said a boy's voice.

I looked up and saw Mark Samson and Davie Kroll standing in front of our table. While Lindsay was impressing us with her knack for remembering statistics, they snuck up on us from behind the soda display.

"This stuff looks lethal," said Mark.

"We must have wandered into the rat poison department!" said Davie.

"That's right," said Lindsay, "but we're not giving out free samples to rats like you two."

Mark and Davie are not only members of the drama club, but co-captains of the soccer team, which makes them the coolest of the cool clique. Most girls think they're the cutest things that ever wore sneakers. They like Mark's wavy blond hair, and Davie's Tom Cruise smile. Even the twins kind of like them. But Lindsay and I are definitely *not* impressed.

Mark's pupils were dilating as he looked at my brownies. "Speaking of free samples," he said, "mind if I taste one?"

"Why would you want to eat rat poison?" asked Lindsay.

"Oh, we were just kidding," said Davie, flashing that "aren't I cute" smile of his.

"But we'd like to have a taste before we spend our hard-earned cash," said Mark.

"No freebies!" insisted Lindsay, but it was too late.

Before we could stop him, Mark snatched up a brownie, broke it in two, and gave half to Davie.

"That will be fifty cents!" insisted Lindsay.

"Okay, okay." Davie slapped two quarters down on the table.

The boys grinned as the brownies neared their mouths, but their happy expressions didn't last long. As soon as they bit into the brownies and began to chew, "Bloough!" Both boys gagged and spit them out. What a mess! Saliva-covered brownie bits flew everywhere! Even my white sweater got hit with soggy flecks of mushed-up chocolate.

"Hey, what's the big idea!" I cried.

"Salt!" stammered Mark as he angrily wiped his mouth on the back of his hand. "Salt! That's what's the matter!"

"Salt?" I said, and nibbled one of the brownies from the bottom of the tray that hadn't been splattered.

The salt flavor was so strong, you could hardly taste the chocolate. I tasted another and then another. All my brownies were laced with salt!

Lindsay's first reaction was to laugh.

"Serves you moochers right," she said.

"What's so funny?" grumbled Davie as he hastily picked up his fifty cents from the table.

"You are!" giggled Lindsay and she started laughing even harder. Then the twins joined in.

Mark's and Davie's expressions were so shocked, so exasperated, so far from their usual cool, I would have laughed, too, but just then I saw Mr. Stillwell and the old lady who let us keep the change coming toward our table.

Apparently our first customer had nibbled one of my brownies while waiting on line at the cash register. Mr. Stillwell was standing nearby. When she gagged on the salty brownies, he wanted to know where she got them.

"There seems to be a problem with the brownies you're selling," announced Mr. Stillwell as he approached our table.

"There certainly is," said Davie, "and they did it on purpose."

"I find that hard to believe," said the old lady. "It must be some kind of accident."

"Accident my eye," said Mark. "It's their warped idea of a practical joke."

I don't think Mark or Davie believed what they were saying. They were just trying to get back at us for laughing at them.

"I'm afraid I'm going to have to ask you to leave . . ." began Mr. Stillwell. "But first you should return this customer's money."

"Well, I guess we're finished here," said Mark smugly, and both boys strode off.

Fortunately, the old woman didn't want her money back. "I'll take some of these cupcakes instead," she said. Then she talked with Mr. Stillwell and convinced him to let us stay.

"I once used baking soda instead of baking powder and ruined a whole batch of biscuits," she told him. "Everyone makes mistakes. In fact, I think you just made a big mistake by asking these young girls to leave."

"Okay, okay! They can stay," Mr. Stillwell relented.

As the old lady was walking away, I ran after her and asked for her address. "I want to send you some of my *good* brownies," I explained.

"Oh, that's okay, dearie," she replied.

"No, really," I insisted. "It would make me feel a lot better."

"Well, You do bake *great* brownies," she said. This time I blushed, but not as much as before. By the time she had written her address in big shaky letters on the back of an envelope, I had composed myself again.

"I'd say those boys back there were trying to get you into trouble," said the old lady as she handed me the envelope. "Did you do anything to provoke them?"

"They did something funny and we laughed," I replied.

"I see," she nodded with a knowing smile. "I guess some things never change."

I had a good feeling inside as I watched that old lady leave the store. I felt proud of myself for the way I had overcome my shyness and talked to her. When I get old, I want to be like her, I thought to myself.

"How did you get the salt mixed up with the sugar?" asked Heather when I returned to the table. "Didn't you taste any of your own brownies?"

"Amy and I pledged not to taste anything we baked," explained Lindsay.

Suddenly I remembered Derrick. I remembered him coming into the kitchen. I remembered him whistling and looking at me with a big smirk on his face. *He* must have switched the sugar and the salt.

"The Avenger!" I said out loud. "The Avenger did it!"

6.
Home Alone

"Where is he?" I hollered, slamming the kitchen door behind me. "Where's Derrick?"

"At Trevor's house," said Mom. "He's staying for dinner."

Coward! I thought to myself. He probably planned it that way so he wouldn't be around when I got home! I put my plate of ruined brownies on the kitchen counter. Instead of throwing them out, I had carried them all the way home for evidence.

"Do you know what that little twerp did?" I said to my mother.

"No, but I have a feeling you're going to tell me." She closed the refrigerator door and sat down on a counter stool. "But before you do that, tell me, how did the bake sale go?"

"Pretty good," I grumbled. "We made almost thirty dollars."

"Is that enough to adopt a whale?" asked my mom.

"It's enough to adopt two whales," I said and sat down on the other side of the counter. Then I told her what Derrick did to my brownies.

"You really shouldn't jump to conclusions," said my mom. Leaning forward, she swung open the cabinet that contained our matching sugar and salt canisters. "It's easy enough to get them confused, especially if you don't read the labels."

"You know, Mom," I said, holding my temper as best I could, "you have the most annoying habit of sticking up for Derrick, even when he's . . ."

"But you could have made a mistake," she began all over again.

"I read the labels on the canisters!" I screeched at her. "I may not be a straight-A student, Mom! But I do know how to read!"

Mom leaned back and heaved a long, drawn-out sigh. "Maybe your father and I should stay home tonight."

"You're going out?"

"Yes, don't you remember?" Mom sighed again. "I told you this morning. Your dad and I are going out to dinner and a movie tonight. Just the two of us. But if you want, we'll stay home and help you get this straightened out with Derrick."

I thought about what that would be like. Derrick would tell his side. I'd tell mine. If I was lucky, he'd say he was sorry. But of course he wouldn't mean it. Two and a half seconds later, he'd go right back to being the creep he always was.

"Thanks, Mom," I said, "but it's not your problem. You guys go out and have a good time. I'll handle Derrick."

"Okay," said Mom, "but please try not to be too hard on your brother. You know he's only eight years old."

"Oh, Mom," I moaned, "I'm so sick of hearing you say that! It used to be, 'He's only four years old. That's why he just spilled nail polish all over your bed.' Then it was, 'He's only five years old, and that's why you can't hit him back when he slugs you with a baseball bat!' Then it was, 'He's only six years old. That's why. . . .' "

While I was talking, Mom glanced up at the kitchen clock. "Oh, no, I'm late!" She slid off her stool. "I was supposed to meet your father ten minutes ago." In a flash she grabbed her coat and ran out the kitchen door. A moment later, the door flew open again. "There's some frozen lasagne on the counter. Just pop it in the microwave. Love ya!" Mom said and was gone again.

"Sometimes I'd like to pop *you* in the microwave," I grumbled out loud.

Then it struck me. With Mom and Dad out of the picture, Derrick and I would be home alone.

I'll bet the little brat didn't count on that!

I ate my lasagne and sat down in front of the kitchen clock watching the minutes tick by and thinking about how sweet this was going to be. Just Derrick and me. For once, justice would be done! "I'll strangle him!" I thought to myself. "No, there are laws against that sort of thing. I'll have to settle for giving him a scare. Yes! That's what he deserves, a taste of his own terrorism!"

I finished my lasagne and cleaned up. As I closed the dishwasher door, I heard Derrick coming up the front steps.

Walking on tiptoe, I positioned myself behind the kitchen door.

I felt like a cat stalking its prey. All my senses were alert, my muscles poised to strike!

The front door creaked.

I heard Derrick's characteristic shuffle on the hall rug.

My moment had arrived.

"You little dweeb!" I jumped out to grab him.

But I made my move too soon. Before I could get near enough to even threaten revenge, Derrick flew up the stairs and escaped into his room.

Click! I heard his door lock from inside.

"You ruined my brownies, didn't you!" I cried, pounding his door with both fists.

"The Avenger did it," replied Derrick.

"But I bought you another Captain Bones!" I cried.

"That spy!" said Derrick. "He was a fake! He didn't know any of Captain Bones's secret codes. I had to destroy him!"

"That hunk of plastic cost me $6.95!" I pounded on the door again. "I'm going to get you for this!"

"No you're not," cried Derrick. "We're even now. If you get me, I'll just get you back worse!"

I pounded on Derrick's door until the back of my hand hurt so much, I had to stop.

"If only I'd been born an only child," I moaned, collapsing to the floor.

Plunger came over and began to lick me. Plunger's the family dog, a Newfoundland with a big sloppy tongue. He got his name because when he licks you, it feels like someone just took a bathroom plunger to your face.

"Get out of here," I said, pulling Plunger closer to me and giving him a big hug.

Sometimes I feel like Plunger's the only one in my family that truly understands me. Whenever I'm down, if I can just manage to spend some time with him, the bad feelings usually go away.

By the time Mom and Dad got home, I was feeling a lot better. Almost okay.

"We decided not to go to the movies after all," said

Mom. "Did you get things straightened out with your brother?"

"Sort of," I mumbled.

"Good," said Dad. "Why don't we all watch this video together? The family that watches TV together is hap-py together!"

Dad's always making up dumb little rhyming slogans like that. I probably shouldn't inflict this on you, but a few of his favorites are: "The family that does dishes together gets their wishes together." "The family that rakes leaves together never grieves together." And, "The family that shovels snow together never feels low together." Pathetic, aren't they? Most of his slogans have to do with encouraging Derrick and me to help him with household chores that he hates even more than we do.

Suddenly Derrick's door crashed open, and he flew down the stairs moving so fast, all I saw was a blur of arms and legs.

"What are we watching?" he cried as he dove onto the living room sofa. Derrick will watch TV until his eyeballs fall out. It doesn't matter what's on. If there was nothing else available, I think he'd watch weather reports all day. He's such a TV addict, Mom and Dad had to put him on a tube diet. Only two hours of TV a day. But videos don't count as part of his two hours.

"It's a classic," said my dad. "It's called *The African Queen*, with Humphrey Bogart."

45

"Oh, good," said Derrick. "I love Humphrey Bogart. He's just like Harrison Ford, only grubbier."

"You coming, Amy?" called my mom.

"No, thanks," I said, remembering the book Lindsay lent me. "I'm going upstairs to read."

7.
Running Scared

The walls to my bedroom may be thin, but when I close my door I feel safe inside, as if they were castle walls, two feet thick and made of stone. I know that sounds like an immature thing to say for someone who's twelve and three quarters, but I really do think of my bedroom as my castle. In my mind there's even a moat. It's just the blue carpet that I keep in front of my door. When I step over it, I enter my own private world. Once I'm in my castle, all I need is a good book and I can shut out the world for hours.

Reading is something Lindsay and I have in common. She always read faster than me. But we used to like all the same books. Sometimes we'd even read out loud together. Lately, though, I've noticed our taste in books has begun to differ. Lindsay's getting more and more into nonfiction. That's why I picked *Sadako and the Thousand Paper Cranes* from Lindsay's cardboard box. Judging from the cover, it looked like the only one that had a story.

I was right. It was a story. A true story about a young Japanese girl whose name was Sadako. Sadako was exposed to radiation from the atomic bomb when she was a baby and died of leukemia many years later. I've read stories about people dying before. But I've never read about anyone my age who died. It was very sad, especially the part about the paper cranes.

One day when Sadako was already sick, someone told her an old Japanese folktale. According to the tale, anyone who folded a thousand paper cranes would get whatever they wished for. Of course Sadako wanted to get well. So she started folding paper cranes. She folded 644 cranes before she died. After her death, her classmates finished folding the rest to make 1,000. Now there's a bronze statue of Sadako in Japan in a place called Peace Park, and the folded paper crane has become an international symbol of peace.

As I finished the last page of *Sadako and the Thousand Paper Cranes*, a strange feeling came over me. I set down the book and closed my eyes. I imagined myself lying in Sadako's hospital bed, dying of leukemia. Suddenly I sensed someone else in the room with me. My mom can walk very quietly sometimes. I thought maybe she had opened the door without my hearing her. I sat up and looked around. But there was no one there.

I got out of bed and went downstairs. My parents and Derrick were watching Katharine Hepburn and

Humphrey Bogart going down the rapids in a battered old steamboat.

"You're missing a great movie," said my dad. "Sit down and watch the ending with us."

"No, thanks," I answered, taking my jacket from the hall closet. "I'm going out for a little walk."

"It's already dark out," said my mom. "Don't stay long."

"Darkness is no problem for Amy," said Derrick. "Vampires love the dark."

As I left the yard, I looked back at the house. I could see the glow of the TV through the living room window. It's fun sometimes to veg out in front of the tube with Mom and Dad. But right now I just wanted to be alone.

There's an old dirt road not far from our house. When I came to it, I turned in and started to jog. As the world rushed past in a smear of murky light, the cool twilight air filled my lungs. I leaned into the night. My strides grew longer. Only the moon surfing along the treetops kept pace with me.

Sadako liked to run. One day she was running a race at school. At the end of the race, she felt dizzy. That was the first sign of her illness. But she didn't tell anyone. She kept the dizzy spells to herself. It was her secret. If I had dizzy spells, I wouldn't keep it a secret. If I had leukemia, I wouldn't fold a thousand paper cranes, either. I'd go to a doctor.

Suddenly all the nervous energy I felt inside of me seemed to drain away. Who was I kidding? If there was a war with nuclear weapons, doctors couldn't help me any more than they were able to help Sadako.

The more I thought about it, the more helpless I felt. Finally I sat down on the side of the road and looked up at the moon. It all seemed so sad and ridiculous. Why did people have to start wars in the first place? What does it ever settle? What does it ever prove? Why can't people just be happy with what they have and live in peace?

When I got back to the house, Derrick had fallen asleep on the living room couch and my parents were in the kitchen fixing a snack. I said good night and went straight to my room.

That night I had a very strange dream.

I dreamed that I was sitting in the living room with my family, watching television. All of a sudden we became weightless, like astronauts in space. We just drifted off our chairs and floated upwards. When we reached the ceiling, we didn't bang our heads. We went right through the second floor, then up and out the roof.

"What's going on?" said Mom.

"I don't know, but it feels good," said Derrick.

"The family that flies together gets wise together," said my dad.

When I looked around me, I saw lots of other people

drifting up out of their houses, too. There were thousands of us all floating up through the clouds and into outer space. Higher and higher we rose, like helium-filled balloons gently drifting skyward, until the earth hung below us like a giant blue-and-white beach ball. To my left I could see the eastern seacoast. To my right, England. The earth turned slowly and majestically beneath me. I saw all of Europe, and part of Asia, too.

Then the figure of a young girl began to drift closer. Though I had never seen this girl before, I knew instantly who she was.

"Sadako!" I cried.

She smiled and reached out her hand to me. I held up my arm and stretched closer. We touched, and I felt her fingers warm against mine.

"You see, I'm not dead," said Sadako. "In fact, I'm very much alive."

Then everyone in space started to hold hands. One by one we reached out to one another, making a giant human chain encircling the earth with love and peace.

8.
The Cool Clique

Lindsay and I have been going to Lincoln School since the fourth grade. Before that, we went to Washington School, which is across the street. That's where Derrick goes now.

Lincoln School is an old brick building with wooden steps cupped and worn from so many students going up and down them since prehistoric times, when dinosaurs used to go there to learn about tar pits (ha-ha, just kidding). Actually, Lincoln School was built during the 1930s. My dad told me it was part of a WPA project to get the country out of the Great Depression, which I think is pretty ironic when you consider how depressing school can be sometimes.

The standard joke about Lincoln School is that it's so ancient, its termites have false teeth. I know it sounds odd, but I really like the fact that Lincoln School is so old. I love its big wooden windows, tall ceilings, and heavy oak doors. Even the molding around the clock in the gym is made of carved oak.

Except for second grade, Lindsay and I were always in the same class. But sixth grade at Lincoln School switches classrooms every period, just like Westfield Junior High. This year Lindsay and I got scheduled with only one class together: math. We can't even eat together, because she has lunch A and I have lunch B. But sometimes we visit between classes and we're always writing notes to one another.

A few days after Christmas vacation, I found a note from Lindsay stuffed in my locker vent:

> Dear Amy,
> Good news! I found an advisor for our Save the Earth Club. Ms. Peterson! I don't know why I didn't think of her sooner. She's really dynamic! We're having our first official meeting today in her room after school.
> See you there,
> Lindsay

As I was putting the note in my book bag, Rachael Harris opened her locker, which happens to be next to mine.

Rachael Harris is a big deal in the drama club, and a core member of the cool clique. Every year she gets a big part in the class play. Rachael wants to be a fashion model someday, and goodness knows she already looks like one: long neck, slim figure, and big, baby-blue eyes. Her mother works for a clothing company, so she gets all her clothes free. It's practically Easter every year before you catch Rachael Harris wearing the same sweater twice.

Normally Rachael doesn't recognize my existence. But ever since I talked to her about joining the drama club, she's taken an interest in me.

"Hi, Amykins," said Rachael. Rachael likes to make up spur-of-the-moment nicknames for people. She thinks they're cute, but I find them obnoxious.

"I got two new CD's this weekend," she said. "The latest and the greatest. Some of the gang are coming by this afternoon. Why don't you drop over? We're going to have a homework party."

"Thanks, Rachael," I said, "but I have a meeting this afternoon."

Even if I didn't have something to do, I wouldn't go to one of Rachael Harris's homework parties. Some of the wild stories people tell about them probably aren't true, but I'm not interested in finding out firsthand. Of course, I didn't tell *her* that. I try to be polite to everyone, even though sometimes it makes me feel like a phony.

Rachael's eyebrows arched. "Too bad," she said. "Mark and Davie will probably drop over for hot chocolate. They always do, you know."

She couldn't imagine why I wasn't thrilled with her invitation.

"Did you hear the latest?" she smoothly changed the subject.

"About Ronnie Liptack and Susan Valani?" I asked.

As far as I knew, the Ronnie Liptack and Susan Valani love story was the hottest rumor at Lincoln School. Last week everyone was talking about how Susan used up two felt-tip pens writing *I love Ronnie* over and over again in her notebook.

"Heck, no," said Rachael. "That's last week's news. Susan's going steady with Dylan Reily now."

"But I thought Susan worshiped the ground Ronnie Liptack walked on," I said. "Didn't you see the notebook?"

I don't follow school gossip too closely. But I try to keep up on the basics.

"She burned it last weekend," said Rachael. "Now she's making a bigger notebook that's going to say *I love Dylan* a *million* times."

"What a disgusting waste of paper!" said Lindsay.

While Rachael and I were talking, Lindsay had come up behind us.

"Someone ought to at least tell her to use recycled paper," said Lindsay. "Did you know that every ton of paper that gets recycled saves eighteen trees?"

Rachael just sighed and rolled her baby-blue eyes.

55

"Well, see you around, Amykins," she said and merged into the crowd milling in the hall.

"I don't think you made a big hit with Rachael," I said, closing my locker door.

"I wasn't trying to," said Lindsay. "Since when are you and Rachael Harris so buddy-buddy?"

"I try to get along with everybody," I replied. "Maybe that's something *you* ought to work on."

Lindsay just shrugged her shoulders. "Did you get my note about Ms. Peterson?"

"Yep, I got it," I replied, "but I still don't understand why we need an advisor."

"Lots of reasons," said Lindsay, "not the least of which is the fact that we need a place to hold meetings at school. Unless you want to meet in the girls' bathroom."

Lindsay definitely had a point there. The girls' bathroom at Lincoln School was messier than the twins' bedroom.

"But why Ms. Peterson?" I asked. "I hear she's kind of flakey."

"Flakey? Ha!" said Lindsay. "Flakey is what most people in this school think *we* are. Besides, I've already checked into it. Ms. Peterson's just about the only teacher around willing to take on a new club in the middle of the school year."

Riiiiinnnnnngggg! The school bell, which happened

to be directly above our heads, rang out like a fire alarm.

"Gotta go," I said and headed toward my home-room.

"See you at the meeting, *Amykins*," Lindsay called out after me.

9.
Good News,
Bad News

Ms. Peterson is the special ed teacher for the entire Westfield region, so she doesn't have a regular classroom at Lincoln School — just a small space in the basement. It used to be the janitor's storage room and still smells faintly of disinfectant and floor wax, but it doesn't look like a storage room anymore. Ms. Peterson covered every square inch of its walls with interesting photographs from magazines and hung a million fish mobiles from the pipes that crisscross the ceiling. The total effect, according to Ruth and Heather, is *hypergroovy*.

When I arrived, Lindsay and the twins were sitting at the low round table that Ms. Peterson uses for her remedial reading groups.

Lindsay was dressed as usual in jeans and an oversized sweatshirt. That's practically a uniform for her. She likes to wear sweatshirts with funny sayings on them. Mostly her dad sends them to her from California.

This one said, "Chocolate, not just for breakfast any-more."

The twins weren't dressed in their hippie clothes, but Ruth's getup was rather wild by Lincoln School standards. Her purple, pink, and black pants, streaked with metallic thread, clashed with the striped Mexican poncho she was wearing. Heather used to dress kind of wild, too, but lately she's been experimenting with a more conservative look. Today she was wearing corduroy slacks and a loose-fitting sweater over a cream-colored blouse.

"We were just talking about world problems," said Lindsay as I pulled up a chair and sat down. "We're trying to figure out what's the worst, number-one, most horrendous crisis facing the planet today."

"Some people think it's global warming," said Ruth, turning the pages of one of the books Lindsay had gotten out of the library for us. This one was entitled *Global Warming: Fact or Fiction?*

Global warming, as you probably already know, is the heating up of the earth's atmosphere from all the carbon dioxide we're putting into the air.

"Unless we do something about global warming," Ruth went on, "good farmland will turn into desert. The ice caps will melt, and places like Florida will be submerged under the sea."

"And poor me!" I said, fluttering my eyelids like a

damsel in distress. "I haven't been to Disney World yet!"

"Other people think the erosion of the ozone layer is the worst problem facing the planet," said Lindsay. "There's already a big hole in it larger than the whole state of New Jersey. If it gets bigger, no one's going to be able to go out in the sun anymore without getting skin cancer."

"Then there's the population explosion," said Ruth, "AIDS, and the destruction of the rain forest."

"What do you think, Amy?" asked Lindsay.

"Little brothers," I said. "That's the biggest problem in the world."

"Come on, Amy," said Lindsay, "we're trying to have a serious discussion here."

"Serious discussion! You've got to be kidding," I said. "What if global warming is the number-one problem in the world? What are *we* going to do about it? Tell everyone to leave their refrigerator doors open?"

"No, smarty-pants," said Lindsay, "but we can talk about it and share ideas about things that *can* be done, like planting trees in regions of the world that are going to need them, and convincing people that we need to reduce air pollution."

"If you ask me, things haven't really changed since the sixties," said Heather. "War is still the biggest problem on the planet today."

"But aren't we finally getting rid of our nuclear bombs?" I said.

"Only to build more sophisticated ones," said Lindsay, "and we're still spending billions on the defense budget every year. Just think of all the good that could be done for the planet if we weren't wasting all that money!"

Just then Ms. Peterson came in the door.

Ms. Peterson is a small, thin woman. She has a round face, and straight brown hair, which is beginning to show flecks of gray. I like the way Ms. Peterson looks. There's a strange delicate quality to her, like an animal from the forest — a fox or a deer.

"Well, ladies," she said, plopping a big pile of papers on her desk. (I loved the way she called us *ladies* right from the start. Though I didn't know it, then, I found out later that she never used that term with any of her other students.) "Since this is our first official meeting together, I'd like to start off with a few general statements. To begin with . . ." She paused as if deciding whether or not to share something personal with us. "I have to confess I almost turned down Lindsay's offer to be your club advisor. You see, I have a very busy schedule this year. And" — she smiled a sly smile — "over Christmas vacation, I got engaged. If all goes as planned, I'll be married this spring."

"Oh, Ms. Peterson! That's terrific!" We all got very noisy with our congratulations.

"So you see, this year is going to be an utterly hectic time for me," said Ms. Peterson when we'd calmed down, "but your idea to have a Save the Earth Club reminded me so much of my college years, I just couldn't refuse."

"Were you a hippie back then?" asked Heather.

"No," answered Ms. Peterson with a sort of wistful tone to her voice. "But I did protest the war in Vietnam."

"Far out!" exclaimed Heather. "Did you ever get arrested?"

"No, I always left before the paddy wagons came," said Ms. Peterson.

At this, Ruth rolled her eyeballs, and Heather pursed her lips.

"But I got wet once when they turned the fire hoses on us," said Ms. Peterson.

Once again, the twins' faces lit up with admiration.

"But back to the matter at hand," continued Ms. Peterson. "What I'm trying to say is, I would very much like to be your club advisor, but after talking to Lindsay this morning, I realized the only way I could handle such a commitment was if you agreed to limit the size of your membership."

I read instant disappointment on Lindsay's face. One moment her eyes were bright and cheery like a puppy's eyes. The next moment they were dull and droopy like the eyes of an old basset hound.

"Limit the size of our group?" she said. "How small were you thinking?"

"Would twenty be small enough?" asked Ruth.

"Much less than that, I'm afraid," replied Ms. Peterson.

"Ten?" suggested Heather.

"Actually, I was thinking of just the four of you," said Ms. Peterson.

"The four of us!" cried Heather. "That's not much of a club!"

"I wanted to start out with four members, not *end up* with that many," grumbled Lindsay.

"I'm sorry to disappoint you so soon." Ms. Peterson sighed. "But I have to recognize my own limitations. If you want to change your minds and ask some other teacher to be your advisor, I understand completely."

"But I've checked. There are no other teachers," said Lindsay. "Anyone who would be interested is already sponsoring a club."

"Then I really don't know what to say." Ms. Peterson sighed again.

For a moment, everyone was silent.

"Well, I certainly don't have a problem with keeping the club small," I said, thinking of how much more relaxed and comfortable I am when all I have to contend with is my friends.

"A small group can still get a lot done," said Ruth.

"It might even be groovier that way," agreed Heather.

"But I was hoping to involve the whole school," said Lindsay.

"There's no reason why you can't do that," said Ms. Peterson. "In fact, I hope you do. Especially for this year's Earth Day celebration."

"Okay," agreed Lindsay. The expression on her face was a pained one. "Maybe next year in seventh grade we'll have a bigger club."

"Good, I'm glad that's settled," said Ms. Peterson, taking out her pen and opening her notebook. "Now let's get down to business. Are you ready to elect officers?"

Although we had talked a lot about the club, the issue of officers hadn't come up.

"Officers?" said Lindsay. "Do we really need officers if there're only four of us?"

"Of course," said Ms. Peterson. "That way, everyone gets to hold a post. President, vice-president, secretary, and treasurer. Any nominations?"

"It was Lindsay's idea," said Heather. "She ought to be president."

That made a lot of sense to me, and Ruth agreed. But Lindsay objected.

"Why can't we all be equal members?" she asked.

"I don't have a problem with that," said Ms. Peterson. "But if you're going to get credit for this club as an extracurricular activity, I have to list officers for the school records."

"We're getting credit for this?" said Ruth. "Far out!"

"Of course," said Ms. Peterson. "It's part of my job description to help students with special interests."

"Well, if that's the case, I'll be president," said Lindsay. "But, really we're all equal members, right?"

"Okay," said Ms. Peterson. "Anyone for vice-president?"

"I'll be secretary," said Ruth.

"And I'll be treasurer," I said, which left Heather with the position of vice-president.

"Will I actually collect dues?" I asked.

"Not necessarily," answered Ms. Peterson. "But Lindsay tells me you've already raised enough money to adopt two whales."

"That's right," said Heather. "We sent the money in last week, but so far we haven't heard from the whale people yet."

"That's a fine start," said Ms. Peterson. "But summer vacation is still a long way off. What else would you like to do?"

"Lots of things," said Lindsay and she ran down a list of possible activities, from planting trees and starting a school recycling center, to writing protest letters to heads of state.

"That's quite a spectrum of projects," said Ms. Peterson. "Is there any focus you can think of that would draw all those activities together, some theme or main event?"

"We were talking about that when you came in," said Lindsay. "We figure there are so many horrible problems in the world, pollution, garbage, overpopulation . . . the list goes on and on. But we're never going to solve any of them until there's peace. So peace on Earth, no more war, that's our focus."

"Sounds reasonable," said Ms. Peterson. "Do you have any specific peace projects in mind?"

"I remember reading about some protesters who broke into a nuclear bomb factory," said Lindsay. "They banged on the nuclear warheads with hammers and poured real blood on them. I'd love to do something dynamic like that."

"Mmm . . ." mused Ms. Peterson. "Although I sometimes wonder about the weird contraptions certain fifth-grade boys build in their desks, I don't think there are any nuclear warheads at Lincoln School we could deface."

Just then my copy of *Sadako and the Thousand Paper Cranes* slid out of my book bag and fell to the floor with a loud slap.

"This is a very good book," said Ms. Peterson as she reached down and picked it up for me.

"You've read it?" I asked.

"Oh, yes," said Ms. Peterson. "It was some years ago. I read it on the train to Washington. I cried all the way from Philadelphia to Baltimore."

"I'd like to read it next," said Heather. Both Ruth and Heather love things that make them cry. And they cry at the oddest things. Like when they go to a horror movie, they *always* cry when the monster gets killed.

"That's it!" exclaimed Lindsay.

"What's it?" asked Ruth.

"Our first project can be *Sadako and the Thousand Paper Cranes*," said Lindsay. "We can go around and read it to every classroom at Lincoln School."

"Can we do that, Ms. Peterson?" asked Heather.

"I don't see why not," replied our advisor. "You wouldn't have to read the entire book from cover to cover — just certain key sections. Then there would be time to have a short discussion afterwards."

"We could even show them how to make paper cranes," said Lindsay.

"How *do* you make paper cranes?" asked Heather.

"It's easy," said Lindsay. "I'll show you how."

"But it will take forever to go into *all* the classes," said Ruth.

"Not if we split up," said Lindsay. "That way, we could cover four classrooms at a time."

It sounded like a neat idea. But the thought of standing up in front of a class and not only reading out loud but conducting a group discussion on my own sent shivers up my spine.

"Ahhhemmm." I cleared my throat and got ready to voice my objection when I noticed a tall, thin man standing in the doorway.

Ms. Peterson noticed him, too.

"Allan," she smiled, "come in. I'd like you to meet some very interesting young ladies."

Of course we all guessed right away that Allan was Ms. Peterson's fiancé. He seemed just right for her. Allan walked over to Ms. Peterson and touched her shoulder with the back of his hand. It was a very unremarkable gesture, almost casual, in fact. But it struck me as very romantic, more so even than a kiss.

"These ladies are having the first meeting of their Save the Earth Club," said Ms. Peterson and she went around the table introducing us all by name.

From the moment Allan walked into the room, Ms. Peterson seemed different. It would be hard to describe the change except to say there was kind of a glow about her.

Allan said hello and asked how things were going. But you could tell he felt pretty uncomfortable around us.

"Well, er . . ." Allan took some tickets from his vest pocket.

"Oh! I totally forgot," Ms. Peterson apologized, explaining that she had to leave soon because Allan was taking her to the theater that evening.

"When can we have another meeting, Ms. Peterson?" asked Lindsay. "Could it be tomorrow?"

"Mmm . . . let's see." Ms. Peterson flipped open her black, wire-bound schedule book. "Fifth period is free for me, and you people have a study hall then, don't you?"

"Yes," said Lindsay, "but we'll need passes to get out of study hall."

"Don't worry about that," said Ms. Peterson. "I'll talk to your teachers."

So that's how our first meeting ended. All in all, I thought it went very well. But I was angry at Lindsay.

10.
My Secret Ambition

"So what's the big idea?" I said to Lindsay as we headed up Glenview Avenue. That's the way we always walk home. I live off Glenview on Baxter, but Lindsay turns off sooner, onto Green.

"Big idea?" asked Lindsay.

"You know the last thing I want to do is get up in front of a class and conduct a *discussion group.*"

"So that's all the thanks I get!" said Lindsay.

"Thanks for what?" I replied.

"Didn't you say you were thinking of joining the drama club?" said Lindsay. "What did you expect to do there, count jelly beans?"

"That's different," I said. "Drama club is all about how to handle yourself in front of people."

"I was just trying to help you with your problem," said Lindsay, cooling down a bit. "But, heck, you don't have to do it all alone. I'm sure Ms. Peterson will let us work in pairs."

That made me feel a little better. As we walked in

silence for a while, I unzipped my coat. In the past few days the weather had gotten a lot warmer. Except for a few patches here and there, all the snow from Christmastime had melted.

"I have a confession to make," I said, holding out my hand to rake the bare branches of a nearby hedge. "Well, not really a confession. It's more like a secret."

"A secret?" Lindsay's ears seemed to grow a little larger.

"Yeah, it's my secret ambition," I said. "So you can't tell anyone ever."

"Cross my heart and hope to die of acne," said Lindsay.

"Okay, here goes," I said. "My secret ambition is to be an actress." Somehow I felt as if I had just bared my soul to the very marrow. But Lindsay's reaction wasn't at all what I thought it would be.

"That's it?" she said, as if somehow I had made a mistake and picked the wrong secret ambition. "An actress?"

"That's it," I said. "Don't you think it's incredible? Me being so shy and all."

"No, not really," said Lindsay. "I think it's called overcompensation."

It's just like Lindsay to use a big word like "overcompensation" when you're having trouble trying to understand her in the first place.

"You know, overcompensation," she went on,

"that's when somebody decides to do the opposite of what their handicap is. Like when someone with polio becomes a marathon runner and wins an Olympic medal. You read about it all the time in the papers."

"Maybe *you* read about it all the time," was my response, "but I've never heard of *overcompensation*. And I'm not handicapped. I'm shy, that's all."

Lindsay kicked a chunk of dirty snow that was lying in the middle of the walk.

"How long have you had this secret ambition?" she asked.

"It depends on how you look at it," I replied. "It feels brand-new, but I guess it's been in the back of my mind for a long time."

"If it's been in your subconscious mind, you've probably been preparing yourself to become an actress all along," said Lindsay.

Now Lindsay was throwing another big word at me: "subconscious" mind. I think I sort of knew what it meant, but I wasn't one hundred percent sure. I'll look that one up when I get home, I thought to myself.

Just then we turned the corner and saw Davie and Mark practicing with their skateboards in front of Mark's house. Looking our way, the two boys flew over the curb and flipped their skateboards up into their hands.

I hate it when boys show off. But I had to admit, when it came to skateboards, Mark and Davie knew what they were doing. Their moves were so quick, it was like watching stuntmen in the movies.

"I hope you're satisfied!" said Mark as we passed by.

There was something so sharp and mean in Mark's tone of voice, I would have kept going, but Lindsay stopped and gave them both a long hard stare: "What in the world are you talking about?"

"Don't look so innocent," said Davie.

"Innocent of *what?*" asked Lindsay.

Davie reached into his pocket and pulled out a yo-yo.

"Of sicking Mrs. Waters on us, that's what!" said Davie, throwing his yo-yo down aggressively. "We got grounded for a whole weekend because Mrs. Waters convinced our mothers that we tried to get you in trouble."

"Mrs. Waters?" said Lindsay, looking at me in dismay.

"The old lady at Shoppers' Choice," I said, remembering the name and address on the scrap of paper she had given me. I had already sent Mrs. Waters the brownies I'd promised.

"Mrs. Waters just happens to play bridge with Mark's grandmother," said Davie, furiously working his yo-yo up and down.

"We didn't put her up to it," I said, trying to smooth things over.

Lindsay's response to the situation was entirely opposite from mine.

"Small world isn't it?" she chuckled with a grin.
"I'm sure you only got what you deserved."

"And someday you're going to get what you de-
serve," said Davie. Raising his arm in a broad sweep,
he let the yo-yo in his hand fly out toward our heads.
I ducked, but Lindsay barely flinched.

"Very funny," she said. "Know any other tricks?"

"I know 'Walk the Dog,' " said Davie and, uncurling
his hand, snapped the yo-yo downward. When the toy
descended as far as its string would allow, he let it
propel itself along the ground. Then he jerked his hand
and reeled it in.

"Hey, that was great," said Mark. "You got it on
the first try that time."

Immensely pleased with himself, Davie grinned.
"Why don't you two take a walk. You're spoiling our
view of that pile of rocks over there!"

I was ready to move on. But Lindsay just stood there
and asked to see Davie's yo-yo. "I have a feeling that
trick was so easy, a baby could have done it," she said.
"Let me try it."

"Not with my designer yo-yo," replied Davie. "See
the insignia and serial number? It's one of a limited
edition."

"Go ahead, let her try," said Mark. "If she wrecks
it, I'll make her buy you a new one."

74

"I guess this is your lucky day," said Davie, pulling the string off his finger and handing the polished wooden yo-yo to Lindsay. "Try not to strangle yourself."

"Thanks," said Lindsay. "I appreciate your concern."

As soon as the yo-yo was installed on her finger, Lindsay let it rip over Davie's head. As he ducked, it went spinning round and round. Then with a flick of her wrist, Lindsay pulled it back. *Thwack!* It sank into her palm.

"That's called 'Around the World,' " she said. "Want to see 'Elevator'?"

Mark and Davie were too cool to let their mouths hang open. But their eyes bugged out while Lindsay performed some really spectacular yo-yo tricks. It was a virtuoso display. The yo-yo was flying everywhere. Lindsay played Cat's Cradle with the string while the yo-yo dipped in and out. At Lindsay's command it dove, it skidded, it bounced. It spun along the ground like a racing car, and then hopped into her hand like a canary. Never once did she lose control.

When she was done, Lindsay slipped the string off her finger and tossed Davie his yo-yo. "Thanks."

For a moment both Davie and Mark seemed at a total loss for words.

It was Davie who finally managed to say something: "That was pretty good for a *girl*."

"Yeah," echoed Mark, "pretty good for a *girl!*"

I could tell Lindsay was annoyed, but she pretended not to care.

"See you around," she said with a carefree wave. But as we walked away, she grumbled, "Boys! Who can figure them out?"

11.
Long-distance Love

So far, I've fallen in love twice. I know it sounds silly, but when I was *really* little I fell in love with Mr. Rogers. No kidding. I even wrote him a letter, begging him to come and live with me in my house. Somehow, I thought he could just climb out of my television set if he really wanted to. Then all he'd have to do is reach in and pull out all his things: his tropical fish, his puppets, his magic screen, his trolley, and all that good stuff would be right there in my living room.

I didn't fall in love again until I was ten. That time my heartthrob was a boy I had met at a trailer camp where we stayed for a weekend on our way to the Grand Canyon. His name was Jeff, and he had the nicest smile. All things being equal, I'm a real sucker for smiles. Of course, I never actually talked to Jeff. I just admired him from a distance. That's my problem, you see. The more I like a boy, the more I feel shy when I'm around him. It's not so bad when there are other people around. But when I'm alone with a boy I like,

I just can't function. I mean, I *really* fall apart.

There was a new boy at Lincoln School I liked a lot. His name was Tony Barlucci. I'll never forget the first day *I ran into him.*

We were both late for homeroom, running down the corridor. When I opened the hall door, *Wham!* Tony smashed right into it, his books flying in every direction.

"You okay?" I asked, picking up his earth science book.

"I think so," he replied, holding his nose and delicately pushing it from side to side. "A little plastic surgery and I'll be as good as new."

Most other boys at Lincoln School would have gotten angry at me for bumping into them like that. "Why don't you watch where you're going!" they would have said, and probably would have called me a klutz or something. But Tony wasn't like that.

"Late for class," he said, and stood up.

"Me, too," I said.

"My name's Tony. What's yours?"

The way Tony smiled at me when he told me his name was just so cute, I couldn't stand it. He was exactly my height, with dark eyes and jet-black hair so curly, it looked like it was getting ready to jump right off his head.

Things had happened so fast, I didn't have a chance to feel shy. But just standing in the hall talking to

Tony with no one else around, I felt myself starting to freeze up inside.

"You're the first person I've run into in this school," he said, picking up the rest of his books. Then he smiled that neat smile again.

"I thought you were new," I said, just to keep the conversation going. "Welcome to Lincoln School."

Welcome to Lincoln School? I thought to myself. What a dumb thing to say.

"Thanks," said Tony, apparently choosing to overlook the fact that I was acting like a complete nerd. "See you around," and he took off down the hall.

I couldn't believe it. I actually talked to a boy I liked without biting my tongue and bleeding all over myself. Utterly amazing!

Then I remembered that Tony had asked me my name and I hadn't answered.

"My name's Amy," I said, but of course he didn't hear me.

Later that week, Tony showed up in my life science class.

That was the day we dissected worms. Our teacher, Ms. Blum, said it was part of the "scientific process of inquiry." I wonder how scientific Ms. Blum would think it was if some alien from another planet started slicing *her* up just to see what was inside.

"The dissection of worms is usually reserved for the seventh grade," said Ms. Blum as she handed out baby food jars, each one containing a giant night crawler floating in formaldehyde. "But I happened to come across some especially fine specimens in my garden last summer."

I'm glad you didn't find any corpses buried in your garden, I thought to myself as Ms. Blum handed me a jar. Then I looked at the limp worm inside. He looked so pale, so pathetic.

Ms. Blum must have noticed the pained expression on my face.

"If you're feeling squeamish, you can let your partner do the actual cutting," she said.

"I don't have a partner," I told Ms. Blum, but she had already moved down the aisle, passing out more worms.

I carefully unscrewed the lid to the jar. The smell of formaldehyde and the way the worm jiggled when I moved the jar made me want to puke.

I was really thinking of taking an F for worm dissecting when Tony came over and asked me if I would like to be his partner.

"Sure," I replied calmly, but inside I was already starting to tighten up.

At first we didn't say anything to one another. We just followed Ms. Blum's diagrams of worm guts on the blackboard and labeled our drawings accordingly.

Then Tony began to talk. His first subject was worms and fishing. "I've fished in every state but Tennessee and Oklahoma," he said. "My dad has a job that makes him travel a lot. So far, we've never lived more than a year in one place. Last year, we moved four times in nine months." Tony didn't ask me any questions or even look at me much. He just rambled on, switching easily from one subject to another. At first, his talking so much made me feel uncomfortable. But Tony was so nice. After a while, I was able to start talking back to him. In fact, once I got going, I could hardly shut up.

While Ms. Blum went from table to table, showing everyone how to use a scalpel, our conversation roamed from earthworms and fishing to just about everything under the sun, including rock and roll.

"So what's your favorite rock group?" asked Tony.

"The Plastic Ono Band," I answered without a moment's hesitation.

Actually, they were Lindsay's favorite rock group. But I thought it sounded more sophisticated to mention the name of a group that Tony probably had never heard of.

"That must be a new group," he said.

"No, it's an old group," I replied. "In fact, it doesn't exist anymore."

"I've never heard of it. Anyone famous in it?"

"John Lennon," I answered. "It's the group he started after The Beatles broke up."

"The Beatles are okay," he said, "but I like The Stones better."

"You like sixties music?" I asked.

"Sort of," he answered. "My neighbor down the street has lots of early rock-and-roll albums in his basement. He lets me listen to them whenever I want to. John Lennon . . . that's the one who got shot, right?"

"That's right," I said. "Does your neighbor have any Country Joe and the Fish albums by any chance?"

"I seem to remember an album cover with that name," said Tony. "Are they good?"

"They're great," I said, but then I took it back. At least I'm not a total phony. "Actually, I haven't heard them," I said. "What I mean is, my best friend, Lindsay, heard them on the radio once. She said they were great. I was wishing I could buy her one of their albums. But you just can't find that stuff in a regular music store."

Later, when I went over this conversation in my mind, it bothered me how much I talked about Lindsay. I didn't like the way it sounded at all. Every other word was Lindsay this, or my best friend Lindsay that. It made me sound like I was just Lindsay's shadow, like I didn't have a personality of my own.

"I doubt my neighbor would part with any of his old records, no matter how much money you offered him," said Tony. He made a deep cut into Mr. Worm, squirting some worm juice onto my hand. Yuk!

"That's too bad." I wiped my hand with a paper towel. "I was really hoping to find that album for Lindsay's birthday."

"But," said Tony, holding his index finger in the air in a very cute way, "if we bring a blank tape to his house, I'm sure he would let us make a copy."

"Could we really? When?"

"Anytime," said Tony. "As a matter of fact, I'm not doing anything after school today."

This can't be happening to me, I thought to myself. It almost sounds like Tony's asking me for a date. For a split second, I felt absolutely wonderful. Then something inside of me shifted. It was like someone reached in and turned the radio dial of my mind to WSHY. Oh my god! He's asking me for a date!

"Ah . . . er . . . sorry," I said, forcing the words from my mouth as if they were blocks of wood. "I have a meeting today."

One moment I was a normal person. Then suddenly I turned into an ice cube. I'm sure Tony sensed it, because his voice seemed kind of unsteady when he said, "Well, maybe some other time."

Then things went from bad to worse. I got that jittery feeling, the one that makes your hands feel like soggy crackers.

"Maybe," I said, in a tone of voice that sounded like, "No way, buddy!" and packed up my books.

Tony never asked to be my lab partner again. I didn't

blame him. It wasn't what I said so much as the way I acted. I'm sure he thought he did something wrong. It was so stupid. I saw myself doing it, but I just couldn't stop. So many times after that, I thought of things that I could have said to put it right. But I never got up enough nerve to actually say any of them.

So my relationship with Tony turned out to be the same as my love affair with that boy named Jeff. I ended up pining over him from a distance, which made me think I was better off when I was in love with Mr. Rogers.

At least he came into my living room.

12.
Lindsay,
the Lion Tamer

Our next two Save the Earth Club meetings were spent preparing for our classroom presentation of *Sadako and the Thousand Paper Cranes*. While Ms. Peterson coached us from the back of the room, we took turns reading out loud. The twins tended to read too fast. They'd start out fine, but then speed up as they got going.

"Slow and easy," Ms. Peterson kept telling them.

Lindsay's reading style was too loud and overdramatic. "This is not cheerleading," coached Ms. Peterson. "Remember, you're going to be reading in a classroom, not a football field."

My problem was just the opposite from Lindsay's. Although it felt as if I was shouting, Ms. Peterson kept complaining that she couldn't hear me. The more I concentrated on turning up the volume, the more my throat tightened up.

Finally, Ms. Peterson suggested that I "stop thinking about what it's *going* to be like. Just read to us and concentrate on what the words are saying."

That seemed to help a whole lot. When I finished, Ms. Peterson complimented me. "I didn't have to go in front of a class until I had three semesters of teacher's training. Just the thought of all those eyes on me made my heart pound like a jackhammer. But I'm not worried about you ladies at all."

"We're women of the future," said Heather.

"Yeah, we don't get ruffled," said Lindsay. "It's not dynamic."

Whenever I'd practice at home all alone in my room, reading out loud was easy. But at night I kept dreaming about reading in front of a firing squad.

One day I met Ms. Peterson in the hall. She was carrying a slide projector under one arm, and a pile of papers in the other.

"Everything's all set," she said. "We're starting with the fourth grade. Tomorrow you and Lindsay will be going to Miss Stone's class instead of your fifth-period study hall."

"Oh, that's really great," I gulped. "Can I give you a hand with any of that stuff?"

"That's okay," Ms. Peterson smiled. "We teachers are used to carrying a heavy work load."

I was late for my next class, but Ms. Peterson wanted to talk to me.

"You're pretty nervous about this, aren't you?" she said.

"Kind of," I replied.

Ms. Peterson shifted the weight of the slide projector to her hip. "I wish I had some magic advice, Amy. Something that would give you instant confidence and make it easy for you."

"Were you really shy once?" I asked her.

"Terribly shy," she replied. "I still am, in some ways. Not in front of a class anymore, but new situations still make me feel as if I want to run and hide."

"I don't know why I'm so jittery," I told her.

"It's nothing to be ashamed of," she said. "If you do start to tense up, try picturing yourself back in my classroom, reading for your friends."

That little talk with Ms. Peterson helped for a while, but the night before our presentation, I didn't sleep well. At breakfast I was so jumpy, I snapped at Derrick for making rude noises, and accidentally knocked my bowl of Bran-o-Bits on Plunger's head. Of course that didn't faze Plunger in the least. He just licked up the spilt milk.

"Good old Plunger." I gave him a hug. Sometimes I wish I could take Plunger around with me everywhere I go. Then I'd never be nervous or shy.

By the time I left my fourth-period class, the butterflies in my stomach were doing loop-the-loops and figure eights. When I met Lindsay waiting outside Miss Stone's fourth-grade class, I was counting on her self-confidence to bolster me. But she didn't look any better than I felt. Seeing her standing there next to the door was like looking at myself in a mirror. The face was different, but the dread was the same.

"I think I've got stage fright," she said.

"Me, too," I replied.

"It just hit all of a sudden," said Lindsay. "Hopefully, it will go away once we get started."

"I should be so lucky. Did you bring the origami paper?"

"Got it," said Lindsay.

Lindsay was also carrying a metal bucket with some small cardboard boxes inside.

"What's that for?" I asked.

"You'll see," she said. "I was reading something last night and I got this great idea. . . ."

"Oh, no!" I thought to myself. What I needed right then was something familiar and reassuring, like Plunger's head to pet or his big hairy body to hold on to. What I didn't need was one of Lindsay's surprises.

Miss Stone stuck her head out of the classroom door. "We're ready when you are, girls."

Lindsay and I smiled nervously at each other and followed Miss Stone meekly into her classroom.

Miss Stone fits my image of what a woman prison guard should look like. She's a big sturdy woman with dyed platinum-blonde hair so perfectly done up in a bun, it looks like it was painted on to her head.

"Sit up straight, class," she barked like a drill sergeant, and everyone snapped to attention.

A firm believer in correct posture, Miss Stone always looked like she had a two-by-four stuck up the back of her dress.

Miss Stone led us up to the head of the class and wrote our names on the blackboard. "Now I want you all to listen very closely to what Lindsay and Amy have to say to you this afternoon," she said. "You're to give them your undivided attention and follow their instructions to the letter, as if I myself had given them. Is that perfectly understood?" she said, folding her arms across her ample chest, as if that settled the matter.

"Yes, Miss Stone," replied the class in singsong unison.

Miss Stone had the reputation for being one of the strictest teachers at Lincoln School. So we weren't expecting any problems with rowdy fourth graders. But we were counting on Miss Stone staying in the classroom. Unfortunately, she had other plans.

"I'll be in the library having a parent conference, girls," she said. "If you need any assistance, just send someone to fetch me. Not that you'll need to. In my twenty years of teaching, this is one of the most well-behaved classes I've ever had." And with that, she left.

As soon as Miss Stone was out of sight, class Jekyll turned into class Hyde. It was like an explosion. Away went the folded hands and innocent looks and out came the spitballs and paper airplanes. Suddenly, everyone was talking, hanging out of their seats, or running up and down the aisles. Two boys even started punching and kicking one another.

Lindsay and I dealt with them first. We each grabbed a boy by the feet and yanked like two people pulling on a wishbone.

"Make a wish," joked Lindsay. But I wasn't in a joking mood.

"Everyone get in your seats!" I hollered, but my voice got lost in the general racket.

"Quiet down!" I tried again, but no one was listening.

"This isn't working," I said. "We'd better send for Miss Stone."

Lindsay just stood there with her hands on her hips.

"We came here to do something, and by golly we're going to do it," she declared. "We have a right to be heard!"

I was already making for the door, but Lindsay called me back.

"Let me try one more thing," she said and dragged Miss Stone's chair to the center of the room.

Then she stood up on the chair and bellowed, "SHUT UP!"

Suddenly the room got very quiet.

"Okay, that's better," said Lindsay. "Now listen up. I've got something very important to say. If this class settles down, we're going to read you a story." The class cheered and clapped. *Yea! Hurray!* "But if you don't, we're going to call back Miss Stone, and you can have a regular class." *Boo! Hiss!* "So what's it going to be?"

"*Sto-ry! Sto-ry! Sto-ry!*" the class began to chant louder and louder.

"SHUT UP!" Lindsay hollered even louder this time.

It was like watching a lion tamer in the circus. All Lindsay needed was a whip and a chair. Actually, she had a chair. She was standing on it. All she needed was the whip.

While Lindsay was taming the wild, fourth-grade beasts, I got another chair, sat down, opened the book, and began to read: "*Sadako was born to be a runner . . .*"

I read terribly. My voice was shaky, and I went too fast at times, slurring words and mushing sentences together. I forgot everything Ms. Peterson had taught us. But the class was drawn into Sadako's story anyway.

I read for about ten minutes. Then Lindsay took a turn. There were no interruptions. No one got up to go the bathroom. No one needed a drink. Finally, Lindsay read the last words:

"*Already lights were dancing behind her eyes. Sadako slid a thin, trembling hand over to touch the golden crane.*

Life was slipping away from her, but the crane made Sadako feel stronger inside.

"She looked at her flock hanging from the ceiling. As she watched, a light autumn breeze made the birds rustle and sway. They seemed to be alive and flying out through the open window. How beautiful and free they were! Sadako sighed and closed her eyes.

"She never woke up. . . ."

When Lindsay finished, the room was even more silent than when Miss Stone had been there.

Then someone's hand went up in the back row. "Is that a true story?" asked a chubby-faced girl with curly blonde hair.

I was going to answer, but Lindsay spoke first. "What do you think?" she asked.

"I think it's a made-up story," said the curly-haired girl. "The United States may have dropped a bomb on Japan, but I don't think it killed anybody."

"That's very interesting," I said. "What do you think happened when they dropped the bomb?"

"It just made a loud boom to scare them," she said.

A lot of people thought that was very funny.

"How many people think that's what happened?" asked Lindsay.

Several hands went up.

"Well, that's *not* what happened," said Lindsay. "It's estimated that between 70,000 and 100,000 people were killed by the single bomb that was dropped on Hiroshima. But that bomb is small compared to the bombs we have now." Lindsay set the metal bucket that she'd brought with her on the floor. "Now I'd like to show you a demonstration of how many nuclear weapons we have in the world today, and how destructive they are."

"You aren't going to explode an atomic bomb, are you?" asked one of the boys who had been fighting earlier.

"Not today," said Lindsay and she opened one of the cardboard boxes that contained hundreds of tiny pellets. "This BB," she continued, holding one of the pellets between her two fingers, "represents the explosive power of all the bombs that were dropped in World War I, World War II, the Korean War, the Vietnam War, and the Persian Gulf War combined." The BB made a tiny *ping* as it fell into the bucket.

Then Lindsay slowly poured the rest of the BB's into the bucket. The sound they made seemed to fill the entire classroom.

"All these BB's," said Lindsay while still pouring, "represent the explosive power of the nuclear weapons that now exist in the world."

Finishing one box of BB's, Lindsay opened another and another. The class was perfectly quiet except for the sound of the BB's striking the bucket.

"Scientists believe that if these weapons were actually used, they could create a gigantic black cloud that could cover the sun and cause all life on our planet to perish," said Lindsay when the last BB had fallen. "It's called nuclear winter. In the past few years, the United States and the former Soviet Union have begun to dismantle some of these terrible weapons. But there're still too many poised to strike at a moment's notice. Someday kids like you and me are going to be in charge of this planet. So even though you're just fourth graders, it's not too early to start thinking about what we're going to do when it's our turn to take over."

You could sense the impact of Lindsay's words by the stillness of the room. No one moved a muscle. The sober atmosphere that Lindsay had created was so complete, it felt like Miss Stone's entire class had slipped into a deep trance. Then the clock over the door clicked forward, and the spell was broken.

Satisfied with the outcome of her demonstration and speech, Lindsay announced that we had just a few minutes to learn how to fold paper cranes before Miss Stone returned.

Most of the kids seemed interested, but a few started horsing around again.

So far I hadn't even thought about *my problem*.

"Not a sliver of shyness," I said to myself. "Not bad, Amy. Not bad at all."

Then something unfortunate happened. While I was helping a fourth-grade girl with her paper crane, I accidentally kicked over Lindsay's demonstration bucket. Thousands of shiny, copper-colored BB's poured across the central aisle under two rows of desks and bounced off the wall into the doorway.

"No problem," said Lindsay. "There's got to be a broom and dustpan around here somewhere."

It didn't seem like a big deal. But just as we got our hands on a broom, some fourth-grade genius discovered that if you got a running start, you could slide halfway across the classroom on the BB's.

Wheeee! What fun! First a couple of kids tried it. Then more and more joined in. Slipping and sliding, squealing and hollering, they fell all over themselves, knocking over desks and chairs. Lindsay and I tried to restore order, but it was like trying to hold an exploding skyrocket in your hand. By the time Miss Stone returned, her entire class was having a wild sliding party.

"What's going on here?" Miss Stone hollered as she strode into the room, "I want everyone in their seats this very moment, and . . ."

Wump! The windows rattled as Miss Stone's feet flew out from underneath her and she crashed to the floor.

13.
Mini-Meeting

After our presentation, Lindsay and I met Ruth and Heather in the hall coming out of Mr. Denton's class. Instead of going back to study hall, we ducked into the girls' bathroom for a quick mini-meeting. As usual, the place was a mess. The sinks looked as if they hadn't been washed since the school was built. The janitor had used lots of pine scent to mop down the floors, but the only fresh thing about the place was the graffiti on the walls.

"We were a hit!" cried Ruth as soon as the bathroom door closed behind us.

"It wasn't us," said Heather. "It was Sadako. They *loved* her. Even the boys."

"How did it go with you two?" asked Ruth.

"Well," Lindsay giggled, "we left them rolling in the aisles."

Then Lindsay and I had a laughing fit that wouldn't stop. We laughed so hard that Ruth and Heather started laughing, too, even though they didn't know what they were laughing about.

"Tell us! Tell us!" they cried. "What's so funny? Why are we laughing?"

I managed to get myself under control just long enough to tell them what had happened with Miss Stone and the BB's.

"Was she hurt?" asked Ruth.

"Only her pride," said Lindsay, slapping her bottom, and we cracked up all over again. Then someone got the idea to flush the toilets to cover the noise. But that only made us laugh harder. I don't think we'd laughed so much since the pajama party at the twins' house when we all decided to brush each other's teeth at the same time.

Then Lindsay pulled herself up onto one of the toilet stall partitions. Perched above our heads, she squatted on the horizontal support beams over the toilet door. "Well, ladies," she began, "if I knew having a Save the Earth Club was going to be this much fun, I would have started one in third grade!" Lindsay had a gleam in her eyes that looked like something out of a Steven Spielberg movie.

"Right on!" cried Ruth and Heather.

"And this is only the beginning." Lindsay pumped her arms with clenched fists. "Someday everyone will know about Sadako. There won't be any more wars. Instead of fighting wars, everyone will fight to save the earth from pollution, drugs, crime, and starvation!"

"Right on!" we all cheered.

"And don't forget overpopulation!" said Heather.

"And the greenhouse effect, and too much garbage, and the ozone layer, and AIDS, and the destruction of the rain forest, too!" bellowed Lindsay. "Maybe we can't do it all on our own. But we can do our part, and maybe our part will add that extra-dynamic something that actually saves the earth from destruction!"

It almost felt as if Lindsay was giving a political speech. It was easy to imagine her sometime in the future addressing thousands. Maybe someday she would even be famous like Mother Teresa or Martin Luther King. I wondered if we'd still be friends then, or if I'd just be part of her past. Someone who could say: "I knew her when she liked to perch on toilet stalls."

Finally, Lindsay jumped down. We all did the peace handshake and began to sing: "All we are saying, is give *Earth* a chance!"

The melody was John Lennon's, but the change of words just came to us spontaneously. Our singing started out loud and got louder. By the time the bell rang to change classes, we had built up so much momentum, we couldn't stop. To just meekly walk out of the girls' room like four ordinary sixth-grade girls was impossible. Without anyone saying what to do, we all joined hands and marched out the door, singing at the top of our lungs: *"All we are saying, is give Earth a chance!"*

14.
Lindsay Out on a Limb

I guess I should have been happy. Compared to Lindsay's other great ideas, our Save the Earth Club was turning out to be a fantastic success. Maybe I'm just a world-class worrier. My dad once said that if worrying were an Olympic sport, I could win a gold medal. I guess being a worrywart comes with my being so shy. The way I see it, that's what shyness is really all about. Worrying that people aren't going to like you. Well, sometimes I do my best worrying when things are going great. But this time I wasn't worried about me. I was worried about Lindsay. It seemed like the more successful we got, the more extreme she became.

Lindsay's always been a radical sort of person. After that speech in the girls' bathroom, her behavior started to border on the unbearable. I'll admit the club helped me feel special, but Lindsay went several steps beyond that. Her attitude became so arrogant, after a while hardly anyone but the twins and me could stand being around her. I could give you lots of little examples:

like the way she started flashing the peace sign to everyone she'd meet in the hall; and how she was always spouting environmental statistics and slogans, no matter what else was going on. Unfortunately, that kind of thing was minor compared to what happened in math class.

As I mentioned earlier, Lindsay and I had the same teacher for math, Mr. Davis. Mr. Davis is a small, baldheaded man who likes to run an orderly classroom. When the bell rings, for instance, he makes the entire class sit perfectly still before he'll dismiss anyone. As teachers go, he's not much fun, but he's fair and I've never known him to be mean.

At the beginning of the year, Mr. Davis gave us a special assignment for extra credit. The assignment was to make up five math questions based on real facts. Every day at the beginning of class, Mr. Davis would ask if anyone wanted to write their questions on the blackboard.

Well, one day when he asked, Lindsay's hand shot up so fast, I thought she was going to put her arm out of joint.

"Okay, Lindsay," said Mr. Davis, "let's see what it is you're so anxious to share with everyone."

I knew Lindsay was up to something. She had that look in her eye that said: "Here comes trouble."

Another one of Lindsay's surprises, I said to myself

and sank down into my chair to see how this one was going to turn out.

While Mr. Davis drilled the class in fractions, Lindsay worked behind him, writing her questions in big capital letters on the blackboard:

1. IF THE BOMB THAT WAS DROPPED ON HIROSHIMA KILLED 90,000 PEOPLE IN THE FIRST TEN SECONDS AND THE BOMBS THAT ARE IN EXISTENCE NOW ARE AT LEAST 10 TIMES MORE POWER-FUL, HOW MANY PEOPLE COULD DIE IN THE FIRST 10 SECONDS IF A MODERN BOMB WAS DROPPED ON A MAJOR CITY TODAY?

2. IF THERE ARE ROUGHLY 3 BILLION TONS OF TNT EXPLOSIVES IN THE MILI-TARY ARSENALS IN THE WORLD TODAY, AND THERE ARE 7 BILLION PEOPLE IN THE WORLD, HOW MANY TONS OF TNT EX-PLOSIVES ARE THERE PER PERSON?

3. IF $3 TRILLION IS SPENT ON ARMA-MENTS IN THE COURSE OF A YEAR, THEN HOW MUCH MONEY IS SPENT EVERY MINUTE?

4. IF 60,000 CHILDREN ON THE PLANET EARTH DIE OF STARVATION EACH DAY, HOW MANY CHILDREN DIE OF STARVATION EACH SECOND?

5. IF ONE MISSILE COSTS $2 MILLION, AND IT TAKES $5,000 TO FEED A STARVING CHILD FOR LIFE, HOW MANY CHILDREN'S LIVES COULD BE SAVED WITH THE MONEY IT TAKES TO MAKE ONE MISSILE?

Mr. Davis finished with the math drill and paused for a moment to read Lindsay's questions. He didn't say anything about them. He just asked for a volunteer to come up to the blackboard.

"And don't forget to show your work," he said. "Even a right answer is wrong if you don't show the work."

When all the answers were on the board, Mr. Davis made a few corrections in long division.

"And don't forget what you have to do when your divisor is larger than your dividend," he said. Then he asked for someone to come up and erase Lindsay's questions and write theirs on the board.

No doubt Lindsay had expected Mr. Davis to say something about her questions. Perhaps she was even hoping that he would challenge her statistics so she could prove him wrong. I'm sure she was ready to handle anything he had to say. But Mr. Davis didn't say anything at all. *This*, Lindsay was not prepared to deal with.

"Mr. Davis," said Lindsay, without bothering to raise her hand, "aren't you going to comment on my questions?"

As a rule, Mr. Davis ignores anyone who doesn't raise their hand. This time, he made an exception.

"I beg your pardon," he answered, touching the many thin lines that ran across his forehead. "Number four had a mistake in addition, and number two . . ."

"But what about the questions themselves . . . what they're about?" asked Lindsay.

"Since I don't know the statistics involved," replied Mr. Davis coolly, "I assume your facts are accurate. Now who wants to be next?"

"Facts! Those are more than facts, Mr. Davis," persisted Lindsay. "Those are the horrible realities of the world we live in! I think any human being in their right mind ought to be shocked when they see them. Don't you agree, Mr. Davis?"

"Perhaps so," said Mr. Davis, unable to hide the quiver of exasperation that had crept into his voice. "However, this is a math class, not a course in political science."

"But what's going to happen to the earth if people stay in their own little boxes and ignore the real problems of life?" said Lindsay.

"I think I've made my point already," said Mr. Davis, his voice still .alm, but rising in volume as he went on. "Now who wants to be next?"

Lindsay looked over at me as if she expected me to say something in her defense. But I just sunk deeper into my chair.

Some hands went up.

"Okay, Jason," said Mr. Davis, and Jason Taylor went up to the blackboard and began to erase Lindsay's questions.

Lindsay was so furious, I could see the muscles in her jaw begin to twitch. Finally, she stood up and said in a very loud voice: "Mr. Davis, I think your attitude stinks!"

I don't think anyone else in Lincoln School would have said that to a teacher. At least not to their face.

Mr. Davis's shiny bald head turned a bright Crayola-red.

"Sit down, Lindsay!" he said sternly. "Sit down, or I'm going to send you to Mr. Kelly's office!" Mr. Kelly is the principal of Lincoln School.

"Maybe I'd like to go to Mr. Kelly's office," said Lindsay without a moment's hesitation. "Yes, I think I'd like to go to the office and tell him exactly what

I think of you and your lousy attitude!"

"Okay, Lindsay Morgan, that's all I'm going to take from you today," said Mr. Davis and he wrote out a note for her to take to Mr. Kelly.

Lindsay did not just walk over to Mr. Davis. She stood up, squared her shoulders, and marched over to him. Her eyes flaring with rebellion, Lindsay snatched the note from Mr. Davis's hand, spun on her heels, and strode out of the room.

After Lindsay left, Mr. Davis proceeded with his usual routine as if nothing significant had happened. But you could tell he had been affected. Twice he made mistakes with simple multiplication facts. No one I knew had ever seen Mr. Davis do that before. Lots of kids can make teachers angry. But Lindsay has a way of *unhinging* them!

There were only ten minutes of class time left to the period, but they felt like ten hours to me. All I could think about was how terrible Lindsay must be feeling.

After class I went straight to Mr. Kelly's office and waited for Lindsay to come out.

"What happened?" I asked. "Did you get a detention?"

"No, just a warning," said Lindsay. There was a hard edge to Lindsay's voice. "So where were you today?" she asked.

"Sitting in my seat," I answered.

"I noticed," she replied. "How come you didn't say anything to defend me?"

"Defend you from what? You're the one who attacked Mr. Davis."

"So you think he was right?" said Lindsay.

"Oh, Linds," I sighed. "Come on, I'll walk you to your next class."

"You haven't answered my question," said Lindsay as we wove our way through the crowd in the hall. "Do you think he was right?"

I felt really terrible because this kind of situation keeps coming up again and again with Lindsay and me. She goes out on a limb, and then gets mad at me for not going out there with her to help saw it off.

"Maybe Mr. Davis was right, maybe he wasn't," I told her. "But the fact is, you're getting too pushy about all this."

"Too pushy?" snapped Lindsay. "Children all over the world are starving to death at this very moment, dying of curable diseases like diarrhea, and that's all you're worried about? That I'm getting too pushy?"

"Think of it this way," I said. "Mr. Davis did let you write your questions on the blackboard. Maybe you should have thanked him for that and let him know how much you appreciated it because of how strongly you feel about those facts instead of telling him how *he* should have felt. Nobody likes that. And it doesn't help the world any to get people to hate you. That's the problem in the first place, isn't it? Too much hate in the world?"

By now we had reached Lindsay's class, and the warning bell was ringing.

Lindsay stopped and looked at me. Her eyes seemed cold and dark. "They're destroying our planet!" intoned Lindsay. "Sometimes you just have to get angry!"

"Angry, yes, I agree," I said. "But we can't help the earth much by hurting one another. That's all I'm saying. It just won't work that way!"

"Okay," Lindsay replied coolly, "I can see I'm not getting through to you."

Except for Lindsay and me, the halls were empty.

"I'd better get to my next class. We'll talk about this later," I said.

But we never did.

15.
Kick Me if You're for Peace

Other than Miss Stone's class, the only other group of kids who gave us any real trouble was Mr. Oblotsky's sixth graders.

It was on a Friday, the last day of school before a three-day vacation. Just as we were about to start our program, Mr. Oblotsky was called down to the principal's office to answer an emergency phone call from his wife. Their three-year-old son had "just swallowed a thumbtack!"

"Can you two handle the class on your own?" asked Mr. Oblotsky as he ran toward the door.

Remembering what happened the last time we were left alone with a class, I was about to say, "No way." But Lindsay spoke up first.

"Sure thing," she said.

Even Lindsay should have known better. All four major cool clique members were in Mr. Oblotsky's homeroom: Mark Samson, Davie Kroll, Marlo Dexter, and Rachael Harris. As soon as Mr. Oblotsky left, they started heckling us.

"What's that you said?" they called out as we read. "We can't hear you."

We raised our voices, but they kept shouting, "Read a little louder. We can't hear you!"

Pretty soon it became the cool thing to do. Everyone joined in. "Louder! Louder!" they shouted. Within minutes, the situation degenerated into a full-fledged free-for-all.

Even Lindsay's "Shut up!" at the top of her lungs technique didn't work.

Marlo Dexter just said, "You shouldn't holler like that, Lindsay. It's going to hurt your throat," and everyone cracked up.

Half the class was throwing spitballs at us. It was like standing in the middle of a hailstorm. Spitballs were flying everywhere, bouncing off our clothes and getting stuck in our hair.

"Linds, I've had it," I said, nearly bursting into tears.

But Lindsay's eyes had that steely look. I knew from past experience when she had that look, nothing would stop her. Even if I quit, she would go on.

"Just keep reading," she insisted.

It would have been cowardly to leave her there alone, so I gritted my teeth and read on. After a while, the spitball stockpile ran low. A few kids kept making new ones, but in the end, Lindsay's stubbornness paid off.

"Any questions?" she asked when we had finished reading.

At this point, some kids were ready to take us seriously. But the cool clique wouldn't let them.

Without raising her hand, Marlo asked, "If folding paper cranes really cures cancer, wouldn't the American Cancer Society know about it?"

"Yeah," said Rachael. "How come we haven't seen any headlines in the newspaper: 'Origami Cures Cancer'?"

They were so cruel, even Lindsay was at a loss for words.

"Hey, Lindsay, is it true that you're a hippie freak?" said Mark.

"No, they're not hippie freaks," said Davie. "They're peace jerks."

"Yeah, that's what they are," said Mark and he got out of his chair and started shuffling up and down the aisle with his shoulders hung back and his arms dangling by his side. "Hi! I'm a peace dude! Wanna save the earth?" He flashed the peace sign and grinned. If anyone else acted that lame, it would have grossed everyone out. But as a member of the cool clique, anything Mark did was automatically cool.

Everyone but us laughed at his antics.

Then Davie stood up, held his hand in the air, and extended his three middle fingers.

"See that?" he said. "That stands for W, which means war. Want to do the war handshake?"

"Sure," said Mark and they imitated our peace handshake, chanting, "War War War. Let's have some more more more! and oh, yeah, Remember Pearl Harbor!"

When Mr. Oblotsky came back, the class monitor told him everything that had happened. But Mr. Oblotsky was so relieved that his kid had actually swallowed a Cracker Jack, and not a thumbtack, no one got punished.

Afterwards in the hall on the way to science class, Marlo came up from behind and patted me on the back. "No hard feelings," she said.

I thought it was a rather nice gesture on her part.

"No hard feelings," I said.

But as soon as I walked into science class, everyone started laughing at me.

I didn't know what was going on until Tony Barlucci came up to me and pulled a sign off my back. "I heard you had some trouble in Mr. Oblotsky's class," he said and handed me the sign.

The sign said, "Kick me if you're for peace."

That afternoon at the Save the Earth Club meeting, I showed Ms. Peterson the sign.

Ms. Peterson just sighed. "Unfortunately, just being different is a threat to some people."

"That kind of thing really flips me out," said Ruth.

"It's the cool clique's fault," said Lindsay. "Every once in a while they have to put someone down just to remind themselves how cool they are."

"Maybe it's our fault, too," I suggested. "You can't blame them for disliking the arrogant way some of us have been acting lately."

Judging from the offended look Lindsay shot my way, it was clear she knew who I was talking about.

"Let the cool clique have their fun," said Heather before Lindsay had a chance to respond. "They can't stop us from doing what we're doing, so what's the difference?"

"That's the spirit!" said Ms. Peterson.

The rest of the meeting was spent discussing our next project. We tossed around a couple of ideas, but nothing really got going until Ms. Peterson suggested we work up a skit for next month's talent contest.

"I got it!" exclaimed Lindsay. "We'll do a TV talk show!"

"Doesn't the talent show have to be live entertainment?" I asked.

"Or course," replied Lindsay.

"Then what's the point of making a videotape?"

"Who said anything about making a video?" replied Lindsay. "All we have to do is pretend like we're in a TV studio. One of us can be the talk show host, and the rest of us can be the guests. Then the people in the auditorium become the TV audience. Get it?"

"I not only get it, I love it," squealed Heather. "I want to be the host!"

"Gosh, Lindsay," gasped Ruth. "That really is a *dynamic* idea!"

"I like it, too," replied Ms. Peterson. "But you're going to need a compelling topic to explore if you intend to hold the interest of your audience."

"Yeah, that's right . . ." said Lindsay. "How about nuclear proliferation?"

"What's that?" I asked.

"That's the spread of nuclear weapons to other countries," said Lindsay. "When H-bombs are small enough to fit in suitcases, they'll be all over the place."

"Mmmm . . ." Ms. Peterson thought for a moment. "That's an important topic. But I would try to think of something a little closer to the lives of your audience, something that affects them on an everyday basis."

"Why don't we discuss war toys?" suggested Heather. "Lots of kids still play with them, especially those shoot 'em up video games."

"Groovy!" said Ruth. "I'll play the part of a concerned mother. I know just what clothes I'll wear."

"And I could be a child psychologist who's just written a book about war toys," said Lindsay.

113

Apparently, I was the only one who wasn't excited about the idea.

"I don't want to be a party pooper," I said, "but, personally, I don't think I could do something like that."

"Of course you can," said Lindsay. "You did just fine reading *Sadako*, didn't you?"

. "Reading in front of a class is one thing, but acting out a part in front of the whole school . . . I don't know if I'm ready for that."

"I thought you were a pretty good Munchkin in *The Wizard of Oz*," said Heather.

Heather was referring to the third-grade play. All I did back then was wear a silly Munchkin suit, prance around on stage, and sing a song with lots of other Munchkins.

"That was different," I said, "and, besides, I almost blew the one line I had."

"But you won't have to memorize anything if you're willing to make up your own dialogue as you go along," said Ms. Peterson. "It's called improvisation."

"There, you see," said Ruth. "Nothing to memorize, nothing to forget."

I wanted to say yes really badly, but I was scared. What if I froze up right in the middle of everything? I didn't want to ruin it for everyone else.

"You could model your character on Derrick and be

a kid who likes war toys," said Ruth. "You'll see. It'll be easy."

"Easy for you guys," I said.

"Do it for peace," said Heather.

"And Mother Earth," said Ruth.

"And don't forget your secret ambition," whispered Lindsay with a sly wink.

16.
The Red Squirrel

The idea of improvising dialogue in front of the whole school felt like something only an insane person would do; like stuffing lead weights in your pockets and going for a walk on quicksand. But the more Ms. Peterson talked about it, the more I actually started liking the idea.

"The important thing is to be able to think on your feet," she said. "All you really have to know is who your character is. Do they cross their legs when they sit? What do they do with their hands? Is their voice loud or soft? If you can *think* how they think and *feel* how they feel, you won't have to act at all. You can just *be*."

Since my character was based on Derrick, I started observing him very closely. Of course I've been observing Derrick for years (whether I've wanted to or not). But this was different. Now I was studying him with a purpose. As you might expect, Derrick didn't like it very much.

"Hey, periscope eyes!" he'd say. "Stop staring at me!"

One obvious thing I observed about Derrick was that he was never far away from one of his war toys. They were his constant companions, always in his hands or pockets. Even at the breakfast table he kept one within easy reach. So of course I wanted to borrow a few of his war toys to use as props for my character.

But Derrick is tighter than last year's ice skates when it comes to parting with his things. My general plan was to get on his good side before I popped the question. I started being nice to him in lots of little ways. I didn't complain when he glommed up all the good desserts. I didn't tell on him when he stole the batteries out of the family flashlight for his remote-control attack helicopter. It was difficult, but I even managed not to have a fit when I caught him using my bed sheets to make an army tent.

After about a week of near saintly behavior (on my part, that is), I decided Derrick was softened up enough. It was a quiet Saturday morning. Mom and Dad had gone shopping. I squared my shoulders and went down the hall to Derrick's room.

The crudely lettered sign below the drawing of skull and crossbones on Derrick's door read:

Keep Out, No Admittance, Top Secret. Patrolled By Vicious Guard Dogs, Electric Fence, and Poison

*Darts. No Man's Land, Proceed At Your Own Risk,
Off Limits, Go Away, Trespassers Will Be Shot In
The Head And Buried In The Mud. Death To Those
Who Go Beyond This Point. Go Back! Last Warn-
ing! Stop! This Means You!!*

I knocked, and the door swung open.

"Hi, Derrick," I said in my sweetest big-sister voice.
"How's my favorite little brother?"

Derrick was lying on his stomach, reading a Combat
comic book. With one shrewd glance, he sized me up.

"Whatever it is you want, you can't have it, so go
away, Weird One," he said. "And shut my door on
your way out!"

Derrick was definitely onto my nice-guy approach.
But I had another strategy.

"Yes, sir!" I said with a stiff salute and smart click
of heels. "But, sir! I have one small favor to ask before
I leave, sir! May I be permitted to speak, sir?"

Derrick perked up. "Yes, what is it, Private Weird
One?"

This approach seemed to be working, so I went
straight to the point.

"I was wondering if I could take some of your war
toys to school for a presentation, sir?" I said.

"No way, Private Weird One," he replied, turning
back to his comic book.

"But it's just for a day, sir," I pleaded. "All I need

is a few things. A couple of guns, a rocket launcher, perhaps."

"You don't know the first thing about maintaining a weapon," he said.

"But, Derrick, I'm not going to break any of your toys," I said, dropping my military manner, "and if I do, I'll replace them. Please say yes. Pretty please?" Sometimes begging works.

"No deal," said Derrick. "I know what you're doing. You're just taking them to school to make fun of me."

"No, you've got it all wrong," I said. "I'm going to express your point of view. Really."

"I don't believe you," he said. "Besides, I shouldn't even be talking to the person who crushed Captain Bones. I could be tried for treason and executed on the spot."

"Hey, I thought we were even on that score," I said.

"Too bad," said Derrick.

I was desperate.

"Okay, here's the deal," I said. "You let me take three of your war toys to school, and I'll give you all my desserts for two weeks." Somehow I knew it would come to that. As far as Derrick was concerned, a little bribery went a long way.

"Ice cream, too?" he asked.

"Ice cream, too," I said, "and any candy I get in those two weeks is yours."

I thought for sure he would go for it. But I was

wrong. Maybe he guessed that I was trying to wean myself off sweets anyway.

"No deal," he said.

"How about a whole month of desserts and candy and you can use my hair dryer any time you want."

Derrick only washes his hair under duress, but he likes to use my hair dryer to dry the paint that he uses on his model bombers.

"No deal!"

Just then a small pebble hit Derrick's window. Derrick's friends never knocked on the door or rang the doorbell. I think they considered it unmanly. They just threw stones at the window, or stood out on the front lawn and hollered.

Derrick opened his window. "I'll be right there," he called down and quickly gathered up the weapons he intended to use for that afternoon's maneuvers.

"Okay, you win," I said, following Derrick downstairs to where his friends were waiting in the driveway. "What's your price?"

After greeting his short but well-armed friends, Derrick finally turned to me and said, "Okay, here's the deal. You can take two of my toys that *I* select to school with you. But you have to play with us for the rest of the day."

"That's all, just play with you for the afternoon?" I said.

"That's right," he said, "but you've got to let us

120

take you prisoner and do whatever we say."

"You're not going to torture me, are you?" I asked.

"Just pretend torture," he said. "And we won't even tie you up tight."

"But you have to scream and stuff when we pretend to beat you up," said one of Derrick's friends.

Needless to say, Derrick's offer did not appeal to me, but I saw no alternative. Besides, I thought to myself, this will be a perfect chance to prepare for my part in the skit. By getting to know what makes Derrick and his buddies tick, I'd be finding out more about *my character.*

"Okay," I said, "But you hurt me, and you're going to be in big trouble."

Derrick's buddies were drooling with delight. They immediately took me to their little fort, which they had built in the backyard with lawn chairs, rakes, and an old scrap of paint-splattered canvas tarp. Then they tied me up and told me I was a third-world terrorist.

"Do you know what a third-world terrorist is?" I asked.

"A bad guy with third-degree burns," said one of Derrick's friends. "We have to get you through enemy lines and back to headquarters before your comrades free you."

"Where are my comrades?" I asked.

"There's one right there!" Derrick spun around and fired his machine gun into the air. "Got him!"

In the course of the afternoon, Derrick and his buddies shot several hundred of my imaginary comrades. They also spent a great deal of time trying to get *secret information* out of me.

"Give us the names of your drug-smuggling buddies," they insisted again and again.

"But you just shot them all," I said.

"Those were just peons!" spat Derrick. "We need to know the higher-ups."

"You want me to make up names?" I whispered to Derrick.

"Of course not," said Derrick. "You never tell us, no matter what we do. Bad guys are tough."

Though they didn't actually hurt me at all, Derrick and his buddies enacted all kinds of cruel fantasies to get me to talk. At one point, they went inside and got some raisins.

"You haven't eaten in days." Derrick popped a raisin in his mouth. "Hunger is gnawing a hole in your stomach as big as a football field. You beg for food." Derrick threw a raisin in the air and caught it in his mouth. "But we just laugh! Ha-ha-ha!"

Just then a baby squirrel that had been living in the canvas roof of Derrick's fort fell out of its nest and onto the dirt floor.

It had reddish fur, a scraggly tail, and big brown eyes.

The boys instantly stopped what they were doing and crowded around the little beast.

It was early spring, but very chilly, so the baby squirrel was still in a state of semihibernation. At first he just stayed huddled up in a ball. Then, slowly, he uncurled and looked up at us with those lovable eyes.

It was amazing to see how quickly Derrick and his buddies dropped their tough-guy act.

"Maybe he's sick," suggested one of the boys.

"No, I don't think so, just dazed," said Derrick, and very gently he cupped his hands around the squirrel and put him back in his nest.

Then we all left the fort.

"I guess we can't play in there for a while," said Derrick.

"Not until he wakes up completely and gets stronger," agreed one of his buddies.

It was incredible. One moment Derrick and his friends were acting out mean and violent fantasies, and the next moment they were kind and gentle. I couldn't help thinking that underneath all that macho play they really felt weak and helpless, just like that little red squirrel.

Unable to continue in their fort, the boys moved their war game to the back porch and played for an hour or so more.

Finally Mom called us in for dinner, and they untied

me. I figured my time was pretty well spent. At least, Derrick seemed pleased. Instead of giving me two of his dinkiest toys to take to school, he gave me his very realistic-looking Uzi submachine gun and a terrific flamethrower. He even threw in a few hand grenades as my reward for being what he called "A Good Sport."

17.
Stage Fright

Sometimes being shy is like playing a cat-and-mouse game with yourself. I can be fine for a long time and handle almost any situation that comes up, but then all of a sudden it pounces. That's how it was with the talent show. The night before, I slept fine. No upset stomach or bad dreams. No paranoid thoughts. I didn't even wake up in the middle of the night. The fact that the next day I'd have to *improvise* in front of the whole school didn't bother me in the least. "And why should it?" I said to myself, "I've rehearsed as much as the twins and Lindsay. If they can do it, then so can I. I'm as good as they are! Right?"

As far as I was concerned, my shyness was a thing of the past. Even a threat from The Avenger couldn't unnerve me.

"Break one of these, and you're dead meat," said Derrick when he handed over his war toys at breakfast.

"Don't worry, little brother," I reassured him, "they're safe with me."

"They'd better be," said Derrick. "I'd hate to think what The Avenger would do to you if something were to happen to them."

As I looked at the flamethrower, Uzi submachine gun, and plastic hand grenades in my lap, I could already hear the wisecracks and stupid remarks some kids would make when they saw me carrying them to school: "What's the matter? Some teacher giving you a hard time?" or, "What are you doing after school today, Amy? Robbing a bank?" To avoid all that, I decided to wrap Derrick's war toys in paper. Unfortunately, the only paper I could find wide enough to do the job properly was some leftover Christmas wrapping. So I still got teased. On the way to school and in the hall, I heard the same wisecrack again and again: "Doing your Christmas shopping early this year?"

But the bold, new, *unshy* me wasn't fazed in the least by such remarks. As I strode into homeroom, my confidence surrounded me like a bubble of light. Inside that bubble, nothing could touch me!

Unfortunately, this particular bubble of light wasn't the long-lasting type. On the way to English class, I passed the trophy case in the hall and saw my reflection in the glass. "I look perfectly calm," I said to myself, "perfectly normal. Everything is going to be all right." Then I heard a voice in the middle of my brain say, "Who are you trying to kid?" and my bubble of light and self-confidence popped like an ordinary soap bubble.

I once saw a demonstration on TV of how a nuclear reaction works. They set a thousand mousetraps on the floor of a room. On each mousetrap they put a Ping-Pong ball. Then they threw a single Ping-Pong ball into the room. That sprung one trap and sent another Ping-Pong ball flying into the air. Pretty soon, Ping-Pong balls were flying everywhere, and all the traps were sprung.

My confidence was just like that room full of mousetraps. Once I started questioning myself, Ping-Pong balls of self-doubt went flying everywhere. What if I get up on stage in front of the whole school and say something really stupid? Or, worse yet, what if I choke up and can't say anything at all? What if the audience laughs at me? What if I throw up? What if the audience throws up? The only way I was able to calm myself down, even a little bit, was to keep repeating to myself something that Ms. Peterson had said: "Just *be* your character. Then *you* won't have to be there at all." I must have said that to myself a thousand times over and over again. "Just be Tommy Smith. Just be Tommy Smith, and everything will be all right." Tommy Smith was the name I'd picked for my character.

By the time I got to English class, I was such a mess, Mr. Klein had to call my name three times before I even noticed that he was talking to me. "Earth to Amy," he said. "Is there any chance that you could come down off your cloud long enough to give us an example of a compound verb?"

"Sure," I replied. "The girl *ran* away and *hid* under a rock."

At lunchtime I sat down and stared at my food as if it were a meteorite that had just crashed through the ceiling and landed on my plate.

"Not hungry?" asked Heather as she stuffed her face with a peanut butter-and-jelly sandwich.

"Who can think of eating at a time like this?" I answered.

"Worried about seventh period?" asked Ruth.

That's when the talent show was scheduled, seventh period.

"I thought I was over all my shyness," I said, "but, now, I seem to have reverted to my old insecure self."

"You did just fine at rehearsals," said Ruth. "Really, you were great."

"But that was without an audience," I said. "Sometimes I can know exactly what I want to say, but the words just won't come."

"Don't worry, we're all going to be there," said Heather. "If the cat gets your tongue, we'll cover for you."

"But it can happen when I'm in the middle of a sentence," I said.

"Perfect," said Heather. "Your character is a little kid, and little kids do that all the time."

I knew Ruth and Heather were just trying to be helpful. But they're so different from me. I wanted to make them understand. "Haven't you ever felt so shy that you wanted to die?"

"Sure," said Heather, "but I just wait, and the feeling goes away."

"Slow down and count to ten," said Ruth. "That's what I do."

"But sometimes the feeling just gets worse and worse," I said. "What do you do then?"

"Ever try the old underwear trick?" asked Heather.

"Underwear trick?"

"Yeah, you know, just picture everyone else in their underwear. Works every time," said Heather. "I thought everyone knew that one."

"That gives me an idea," said Ruth. "Wouldn't it be great if we had a national underwear day when everyone came to school in their underwear?"

"I bet Mr. Kelly wears big baggy ones with polka dots," giggled Heather.

"And Mr. Applebaum, the janitor, has a tool belt sewn onto his," said Ruth.

They had funny things to say about everyone's underwear. I laughed so hard, milk went up my nose.

"That's the best medicine for nerves," said Ruth.

"Milk up the nose?" I asked.

"Right," said Heather. "Lots of milk up the nose. Works every time."

129

Although the talent contest was scheduled for seventh period, all the contestants had to report to the auditorium at the beginning of sixth period. We were told to meet backstage. But the person who was supposed to let us in was late.

There was a real mob scene in the hall as we all waited for the backstage door to be opened. Randy Berkowitz was practicing his juggling act dropping beanbags on the floor and muttering to himself. Sara Page was doing *pirouettes* in her tutu. Roxanne Bentworth was silently mouthing the words to the pop tune she was going to sing.

Everyone was trying to look cool, calm, and collected, but only the drama club seemed genuinely relaxed. They were talking among themselves in front of the audiovisual aids closet. Every once in a while Rachael would look over Marlo's shoulder. The bored look on her face seemed to say, "What a shame it is that we have to be surrounded by such lowly specimens of humanity."

"Hey, Amy!" I heard a voice call from behind me. I turned and saw Ruth leaning out of the girls' bathroom. "Come on, we're getting ready in here."

I picked up my gear, left the crowd in the hall, and ducked into the girls' room.

Lindsay was standing in front of the long, horizontal mirror that hung over the sinks, applying some of her mother's lipstick. She was all decked out in her most grown-up looking clothes, a tweed suit with a tan blouse. Her hair was pulled back in a bun, and she was wearing glasses with big heavy frames that made her look very studious. If she weren't so small, she would have looked thirty years old. On the edge of the sink was a history book with a cover that said *War Toys "R" Us*.

"What's that?" I asked.

"That's my latest publication, darling!" said Lindsay in a grown-up sounding voice with a heavy British accent.

"Why are you talking so funny?" I asked.

"Because I was in character," said Lindsay, returning to her normal tone. "I've always thought British accents make people sound more intelligent. I mean, they're so dynamic. Don't you agree?"

"I'd drop the accent," said Heather.

Heather had just emerged from one of the bathroom stalls in a tight-fitting red dress that made her look like a high-society debutante. Weeks ago she'd showed me the dress, but this was the first time I had seen her wearing it. She looked so stunning, I simply had to gasp, "Oh, Heather, you look fabulous!"

"I clink!" she said and raised her arms, which were draped in gobs of her mother's gold jewelry.

Ruth's costume looked like something my grandmother would wear when she's cleaning house. It was a really tacky outfit: a frumpy old flower print dress

131

with an oversized apron. Her hair was done up in old-fashioned hair curlers, and she had a rag wrapped around her forehead.

"How do I look?" she asked. Although Ruth was trying her best to look dumpy, she still looked gorgeous. "I was thinking of bringing in a vacuum cleaner for special effects," she said, "but it was too heavy to carry."

"Oh, that would have been great," said Lindsay. "You could have stopped in the middle of everything and tidied up the stage."

I set down the package containing Derrick's war toys, opened the paper bag I had with me, and took out my costume: a pair of overalls and a baseball cap, which I planned to wear brim side facing backwards.

"Doing your Christmas shopping early this year?" asked Lindsay.

Just as I got my overalls on, Ms. Peterson poked her head in the girls' room.

"So there you are, ladies!" she said. "I've been looking.everywhere for you."

"The stage door was closed," explained Lindsay.

"Well, it's open now," said Ms. Peterson and she escorted us to the auditorium.

Backstage was dark and dusty, with lots of old crates and pieces of scenery stacked up against a bare cinder block wall. Contestants milled about, while stagehands called to one another as they tested lights and ropes.

Beyond the heavy maroon curtain I could hear the shuffling noise of the audience being seated.

Then our principal, Mr. Kelly, came backstage.

"Line up and take a number," he announced and began handing out numbered pieces of paper so we would know when to go on.

Because we had spent so much time in the girls' room, we ended up last in line, number thirteen.

"Just our luck to get number thirteen," said Ruth.

"Thirteen isn't really unlucky," said Lindsay. "In fact, some people think it's very lucky because it's the number of full moons in a year."

"Be ready when your number is called," said Mr. Kelly.

"I'm ready to crawl into a hole," I mumbled to myself, thinking no one could hear me.

But Ms. Peterson responded, "Don't worry, Amy." She patted me on the shoulder. "You're going to do just fine."

"Will your group need any special equipment?" Mr. Kelly asked Ms. Peterson.

"Just some chairs," she answered.

"What a bummer!" exclaimed Ruth. "We forgot the chairs!"

"Don't worry." Ms. Peterson pointed to some folding chairs leaning against the back wall. "I brought them down this morning. When you go out, just take one with you."

While we waited for the show to begin, Lindsay went over her notes. Ruth fussed with her hair curlers. Heather checked out the hand-held microphone that she intended to use, and I unwrapped my war toys.

Finally Mr. Kelly introduced the first act: Marvin Krebs and his comedy routine.

Marvin told *old* elephant jokes, the same ones we all heard in third grade. He got quite a few laughs. Not for the jokes, but for the funny, high-pitched cackle he delivered with each punch line.

Then it was Edna Sardinsky's turn. She did an acrobatic routine to Stravinsky's *Firebird Suite*. Except for falling down twice, she was quite good. She got some applause, anyway. And so did Martin Shorner and his saxophone solo. Ellen Yellers also did pretty well with her pantomime of someone going grocery shopping. At least the part where she ate a banana and then slipped on the peel got a few laughs.

Of course the drama club's presentation was outstanding. They did a scene from *A Midsummer Night's Dream*. You wouldn't think that the students of Lincoln School would like Shakespeare so much, but they did. The old bard came up with some really funny material, and the drama club put it across with pizzazz. I have to give them credit for doing a terrific job. Davie was especially good as Puck, and Rachael's Queen of the Fairies was impressive.

The auditorium was still echoing with applause as

they came backstage. Rachael and Marlo looked absolutely radiant in their silvery gowns.

"Well, I guess that decides who won this year's contest," said Davie.

"It really wasn't fair," said Rachael. "No one else had a chance."

"It's not our fault we're so good," said Marlo.

Lindsay didn't say anything to the triumphant cool clique as they strutted past us, but the look of hate she sent their way seemed powerful enough to set their clothes on fire.

"Contrary to what some people think, this contest is not over yet," she muttered to us through clenched teeth.

After the cool clique, it was Howard Morton's turn. Although I don't know a warbler from a wren, I thought his bird imitations sounded pretty convincing. But he didn't get very much applause.

"It wasn't poor Howard's fault," I heard Marlo whisper to Rachael. "We're just too hard of an act to follow."

Then Mr. Kelly stuck his head backstage: "Number thirteen!"

"That's us," said Lindsay. "Everybody ready?"

"Ready to die," I muttered to myself and plunged through the curtain onto the stage.

18.
"This Is Going to Be Great!"

I avoided the many-eyed monster that was the audience. I looked only at my hands, or focused on the hardwood floor beneath my feet. Meaningless details like the wad of old gum stuck to the bottom of my chair grabbed hold of my attention and filled the numbness that my mind had become. I felt separate from my body. Whether it belonged to someone else or to no one at all, I couldn't tell. I watched my hands put the war toys on the floor next to the leg of my chair. Then I waited robotlike while my fingers laced themselves together like the two sides of a zipper.

Lindsay reached over and touched me on the leg.

"This is going to be great," she said. "Can you feel it? There's a kind of electricity in the air."

"Yeah," I replied, "the kind they use to electrocute people."

Then Heather stood up and began to talk into her microphone.

"Good evening, ladies and gentlemen in the studio

audience, and you watching at home . . ." She let the words roll off her tongue like a real TV talk show host. ". . . And welcome to *Today's Talk*, the television show that's not afraid to talk about what America really thinks. I'm your host, Lydia MacMillions, and tonight we are going to discuss war toys! Are they harmless, or should they be banned?"

Heather was really good. From the moment she opened her mouth, she had the audience paying attention to her every word. "And now I will introduce our guests. To my immediate right is the well-known child psychologist and syndicated columnist, Amanda Richfield." Lindsay nodded and held up a copy of her new book, *War Toys "R" Us*, for the studio audience to see.

"I'm very pleased to be here tonight," said Lindsay, "and I hope you all get a chance to go out and buy my new book. It costs $14.95, but when the paperback comes out it will be a lot less expensive. It's all about war toys and why . . ."

Lindsay was playing her character just the way she said she would: self-centered and pushy.

"Yes, yes, thank you," said Heather. "We'll want to hear more from you later on in the show, but now I'd like to introduce the rest of tonight's guests."

Then Heather began to introduce me. There's no turning back now, I thought. When she's finished, I'm going to have to say something.

While Heather spoke, my thoughts got stuck somewhere between panic and confusion. Should I use these last few seconds to figure out what I'm going to say, or should I just sit here and trust that inspiration will come?

Heather finished, and I still hadn't gotten up enough courage to *look* at the audience. This is it! I thought. The worst is happening. A complete disaster!

I heard the pounding rhythm of a bass drum, and I remember saying to myself, "Whoever is playing that drum, I wish they'd stop it." Then I realized it was the pounding of my own heart that I was hearing. Somehow that snapped me out of it.

I stood up, squared my shoulders, lifted my plastic machine gun, and let the words fly out of my mouth: "So let's get on with the show!" It was the macho kind of thing that Derrick or one of his friends would have said. I was mortified, but the audience seemed to like it. At least they laughed. So far, so good.

Heather's opening question was, "What's really so terrible about war toys and the cartoons that advertise them?"

Lindsay jumped right in, quoting facts and studies about the effects of war toys and how they make little kids act more violently.

"Did you know that a typical Saturday morning cartoon contains six deaths per minute?" she began. "Studies show conclusively that witnessing all that

138

killing has a negative effect on young minds, especially when there's violence in the home."

Thinking of what Derrick might have said, I objected. "But those are just pretend deaths. What you grown-ups seem to forget is that we kids know the difference between real life and make-believe."

"Oh, really?" said Lindsay. "Then how come studies have shown that kids who watch Saturday morning cartoons are ten times more likely to engage in violent play?"

Then Ruth got involved. "My youngest child is only four years old," she said, "and he can't tell the difference between the cartoons and the advertisements."

"So maybe your kid isn't too bright!" I countered. "Besides, this is a free country. People have a right to watch whatever they want, don't they? Take this show, for example. I think it's boring. If I were at home, I'd turn the channel and watch something else!"

That got a pretty good rise out of the audience. Our strategy of attempting to express both sides of the war toy controversy was working even better than we had planned.

"Of course this is a free country," responded Ruth, "but we parents have a responsibility to our children. My Gregory would eat cake and ice cream five times a day if I let him. But I don't, because it's unhealthy and rots his teeth. Well, I think war toys rot kids' minds, just like sugar rots their teeth."

Ruth played with her hair curlers while she spoke. Every once in a while, one would pop off her head and roll onto the floor. Every time that happened, she made a funny face that sent ripples of giggles through the audience.

"Of course, some sweets like the sugars in fruit aren't such a terrible thing," she continued. "That's why I don't mind if my children make their own war toys. I let them make guns out of old scraps of wood and things like that. I just don't want a multimillion-dollar industry selling them violence any more than I want drug pushers selling them drugs!"

"And it's not so much the toys themselves," said Lindsay. "It's the way they're sold that's so destructive. By the age of eighteen, the average child in the United States will have seen between 350,000 and 640,000 television commercials. Many of the cartoon programs are really half-hour commercials that make little kids think the world is full of bad guys and that the only way to solve the world's problems is by violence."

"But the world *is* full of bad guys!" I said. "What do you want to do? Outlaw war toys?"

"They're already illegal in some countries," replied Lindsay.

"Hold on," I said. "War toys are good for me. See this machine gun?" I pointed my machine gun right at the audience. "When I'm angry at my mom for making me clean my room or something, I can go out and pretend to fry a whole battalion of enemy soldiers. *Bam! Bam! Bam!* It makes me feel a lot better. If kids didn't have war toys, they'd turn into wimps!"

"But there are much healthier ways to help young boys come to terms with their aggressive feelings," said Lindsay. "Instead of wasting our money on things that teach war as a way of solving problems, we ought to be teaching our kids that war is the biggest problem in the world today!"

Lindsay wasn't using her Amanda Richfield voice anymore.

"Don't get me wrong," she said, launching into a long and passionate speech, "I'm not against kids having fun. I'm against grown-ups teaching kids the *fun* of killing. It's insane! Utterly insane. And who's suffering for it? We all are. You, me, and everybody else! Just look at what happened with the Persian Gulf War. Over a hundred thousand people were slaughtered! Billions of dollars of damage was done to the environment, and the media made the whole thing look like one giant video game!"

It was just like that time in the girls' bathroom when Lindsay stood up on the toilet stall. Only now she was standing up in front of the whole school. "The animals are dying, the forests are burning, the water is dirty, the air isn't going to be fit to breathe, and our soldiers come marching home like heroes! Well, I say there aren't going to be any real heroes until this planet is

141

snatched back from the hands of the warmongers!"

Lindsay was just terrific.

"Now's the time for everyone to put down their weapons, even if they're just toy guns," she said. "We all have to roll up our sleeves and save the earth for ourselves, our children, and our children's children. . . ."

There was some kind of hypnotic force flowing out of Lindsay and into the audience. I don't know how to describe it except to say that it really was dynamic. Listening to her, I got inspired all over again!

We had talked about how we were going to end our presentation. Heather was going to thank the contestants and cut to a commercial. But we never got a chance to do that. When Lindsay finished, the whole auditorium exploded into wild applause!

Everyone backstage was applauding, too; everyone, that is, except the cool clique.

19.
Some Surprise!

Our prize for winning the talent contest was a free coupon for two large Pizza Boy pizzas. The twins and I wanted to cash them in right away. But Lindsay convinced us all to wait until the weekend.

"It will be more dynamic that way," she insisted. As it turned out, we had to wait a lot longer than the weekend.

The very next day something terrible happened.

I walked to school that morning, still basking in the warm glow from yesterday's victory. Not only had I done a good job, but we had actually won! I still couldn't believe it. I kept replaying our victory in my mind as if I were watching and rewinding an old video over and over again. Unfortunately, some parts of that video needed editing.

When Mr. Kelly announced that we had won, I noticed a tiny tear ooze out of one of Rachael Harris's baby-blue eyes.

"There must be some mistake!" she sobbed.

"Don't feel bad," said Lindsay. "We're a hard act to follow."

"I wouldn't act so stuck-up if I were you, Turbo Tongue!" hissed Marlo.

"And I wouldn't act at all if I were you," snapped Lindsay.

"I hope you guys choke on that pizza," said Davie.

This time, Lindsay didn't reply. She didn't have to. The cool clique had completely blown its cool.

As I approached Lincoln School, I noticed a large crowd of kids milling around the main entrance. I ambled over to check out what was happening.

Then I saw it! Someone had taken a can of red spray paint and written across the front door of the school in big scrawly letters:

Mr. Davis is a Warmonger!

For a moment I just couldn't connect with what my eyes were seeing. Mr. Davis, my math teacher, a warmonger? Who would write such a thing? Then I heard someone standing next to me say, "Looks like your fanatical friend went a little too far this time."

I was too embarrassed to even turn around to see who had spoken. I just pushed through the crowd and went straight to Lindsay's homeroom.

"Have you seen Lindsay?" I asked Tad Green, whose desk is next to Lindsay's. As soon as I asked, I knew

I had made a mistake. Tad's not exactly in the same reality as everyone else. Somehow he manages to get passing grades, but most of the time he just sits in class all day, designing perpetual motion machines.

"Lindsay who?" he said. He's only been sitting next to Lindsay since September.

Then Mr. Fletcher, Lindsay's homeroom teacher, came in the door. "If you're looking for Lindsay," he said, "she's already been sent home."

"Oh, I see." I tried to sound as casual as possible.

Leaving Lindsay's homeroom, I saw the twins marching down the hall.

"Have you heard?" asked Heather.

"Yes," I nodded, and we all just stood there for a moment, exchanging helpless looks.

"What a downer!" said Ruth. "I can't believe this is happening."

"Have you seen Lindsay?" I asked.

"Just for a moment, when she left Mr. Kelly's office," said Heather. "She said she was suspended for two weeks and our Save the Earth Club has been canceled."

"Canceled!" I gasped.

"Like a stamp," said Heather.

"Or a baseball game," said Ruth.

"They can't get away with this," I said. "Let's go talk to Ms. Peterson about this."

"Not possible," said Heather. "Today's Tuesday. She's at Willamsburg School."

"I can't believe Lindsay did this," said Heather. "But I heard someone *saw* her do it."

"Did she tell you she was going to do it?" Ruth asked me.

"No," I replied, "but you know how Lindsay loves surprises."

"Some surprise," said Heather.

The first thing I did after school that day was call Lindsay's house, but her line was busy for hours. I would have gone straight over to see her, but I had to stay home and baby-sit for Derrick. It seemed like such a useless task. If there was ever an eight-year-old who could take care of himself, it was Derrick. Of course Mom and Dad didn't see it that way.

"Wings in a Bucket for dinner," announced my dad as he came in the front door. "The family that dines together binds together!"

I helped Mom make a salad, while Dad and Derrick set the table.

"How did things go at school today?" asked my mom as she mixed up some salad dressing.

I was tempted to tell her the whole story, but I decided to wait until I talked to Lindsay first.

"Okay, I guess," I answered.

Later as we sat down at the table, Dad cleared his throat. "Hrumph . . . er . . . Amy." He opened the bucket of chicken wings. "I've been worried about you lately."

"*Moi?*" I responded.

"That's right," he replied. "Gary told me some disturbing news today."

Sometimes I think Einstein was wrong. There is something that can travel faster than the speed of light: bad news. Gary is a guy that works with my dad at the office. His son, Mel, is one of Lincoln School's most notorious troublemakers. His speciality is lighting firecrackers on the playground. But of course Gary doesn't talk much about that.

"What's Pain in the Butt done now?" asked Derrick.

"Watch your language, young man!" snapped my mom.

"It's just military talk, Mom," said Derrick. "You wouldn't understand."

"I understand that you can take your dinner up to your room and eat by yourself," said my dad.

As he slid off his chair, Derrick favored Dad with one of his meaner tough-guy looks. "These K rations aren't any good tonight, anyway," he said.

Now that Derrick was out of earshot, Mom and Dad started firing questions at me like two cops giving a suspect the third degree.

"I understand Lindsay was suspended from school today for defiling public property. You didn't have anything to do with it, did you?" asked my mom.

"Of course not," I said, "but . . ."

"Is it true that you and your friends make pests out of yourselves and march down the halls holding hands and chanting at the top of your lungs?" inquired my dad.

"Well . . ." I began, but Mom didn't let me finish.

"And what about this cult handshake?" she pressed.

"Cult handshake!" I protested. "Gosh, Mom, you make it sound like we're all on drugs or something!"

"Well?" asked my mom.

"Well what?" I said.

"Have you or your friends ever taken any drugs?" she asked.

I just couldn't believe it!

My own mother was asking me if I took drugs!

To think she didn't know me any better than that!

"Mom!" I hollered, *"I don't take drugs!"*

"Drugs are a very big problem these days, even with children your age," said my dad. "You can't blame us for worrying about you."

"But we all hate drugs. Drugs are what killed the hippie movement. Janis Joplin, Jimi Hendrix, Jim Morrison. They'd all still be alive today if it weren't for drugs," I said, quoting something Lindsay had once said.

"There, you see," said my mom, throwing down her

napkin. "That's all they think about, hippies, bell-bottoms, and rock and roll!"

"Rock and roll!" I said. "How can you object to that? It's the music of your own generation. You told me yourself that you used to listen to it all the time!"

"Don't change the subject," said Mom. "Besides, we were young then."

"Well, I'm young now."

"We just don't want you to do anything you might regret," said my dad.

"Then I might as well not do anything at all."

"No fresh comments, please!" snapped my mother. "Remember, the most important thing about school is getting good grades."

So it's grades again, is it? I thought to myself, Why do they always say the same things? Next they'll start talking to me about college.

"It's getting harder and harder to get into college," said my dad. "If you fall back this year, you could fall even farther behind next year."

"We're worried about you, dear," said my mom. "We just want you to do what's right."

"As a matter of fact, I do have lots of homework tonight," I said. "May I be excused?"

Mom and Dad looked at one another.

"Yes, you're excused," said my dad. "But I want you to think about what we said."

"And I want you to think about what I said," I muttered under my breath as I left the table.

"What's that?" said my dad.

"Nothing," I said, but I think he heard every word.

On the way through the living room, I picked up the remote phone and carried it up to my bedroom.

Lindsay's phone rang only once.

"Oh, Amy," she gasped, "I'm so glad it's you."

"I've been trying to call you all day," I said.

"Mom made me take the phone off the hook," said Lindsay. "She says she's too embarrassed to talk to anyone right now."

"Why didn't you call me?" I asked.

"I'm grounded so bad, I practically have to ask permission to go to the bathroom," explained Lindsay. "But we çan talk now. Mom just left to go to the store for some milk. She said I couldn't *make* any phone calls. She didn't say anything about answering them."

Lindsay's voice sounded desperate, but I couldn't hold back my feelings any longer.

"I hope you realize what a rotten mess you've gotten us into!" I lit into her. "Mr. Kelly's canceled our club, and . . ."

"But I didn't do it!" said Lindsay.

"I tried to warn you, but no. You wouldn't listen," I said. "Then you go and pull a stupid stunt like this. And you're supposed to be the smart one. Ha!"

"But Amy, *I didn't do it!*" said Lindsay.

"You're the dynamic one. Well, let's see you dynamic yourself out of this one!" I said.

"I said I didn't do it!" Lindsay was shouting now. Finally I heard her.

"You didn't do it?"

"No way," said Lindsay. "I can't blame you for thinking I did. Even my mother doesn't believe me."

"But someone saw you do it," I said.

"Someone lied," said Lindsay.

"You really, really didn't do it?" I said.

"I *really, really, really* didn't do it!" insisted Lindsay.

"Then how come you got suspended?" I said.

"Mr. Kelly was very rude to me," said Lindsay. "He ranted and raved and never gave me a chance to defend myself. I ended up calling him a jerk."

"But he can't just cancel our club without some kind of warning."

"He did give us a warning," said Lindsay, lowering her voice to a whisper. "When I got sent down to his office by Mr. Davis, Mr. Kelly said that if we made any more trouble for him, he'd cancel the club and all our activities."

"You never told me," I said. "You should have told me that!"

"Maybe if you had gotten sent down to Mr. Kelly's office, you would have heard him say it yourself!" snapped Lindsay.

I couldn't believe Lindsay was still holding that

against me. Part of me wanted to hang up on her right then and there. But I let it go. If ever there was a time Lindsay needed a friend, it was now.

"So what are we going to do?" I asked.

"Don't worry. I'll think of something," she said. "Uh-oh! Mom's home. Come on over tomorrow after school. And bring the twins!" Click!

I was so spaced. For a long time I just sat there, holding the phone in my hand. Finally a recording came on and told me to hang up and dial again.

20.
Worst Kind of Wimp

"*I*'ve been waiting all day to talk to you guys," said Lindsay as soon as we came in the door.

Lindsay had traded in her jeans and T-shirt for an outfit of black pants and a black blouse. It was the first time I had seen her dressed completely in black. But not the last. As time passed, "the funeral look," as Ruth called it, was something Lindsay would wear more and more often.

Lindsay was sitting on her bed letting Marvin climb on her head. While we talked, he roamed through her hair, poking his nose out occasionally to sniff the air.

"So who was it?" Lindsay wasted no time getting down to business. "Who was the dirty liar who said they saw me defacing school property?"

"We asked around everywhere," said Ruth, plopping herself down on Lindsay's bed.

"Not so rough," said Lindsay. "You'll scare Marvin."

"Rumor has it that Mr. Kelly received an anonymous phone call," said Heather. "But it's just a rumor. I

153

don't think there's any truth to it at all."

"Of course there isn't," said Lindsay. "But it just goes to prove that I was set up. Whoever started that rumor wanted to get me in trouble."

"The cool clique?" asked Heather.

"Who else could it be?" said Lindsay. "They couldn't take losing the talent contest, so they set me up just for spite!"

"Right on," said Ruth, "but how are we going to prove it?"

"Here's my plan," said Lindsay.

"See, I told you Lindsay would have a great idea ready and waiting when we got here," said Heather.

"I'm going home now," I said and stood up to leave.

"Very funny," said Lindsay. "Now sit down and listen to what I have to say. This isn't as difficult a situation as you think. In fact, the solution turns out to be very simple."

"Isn't it always?" I groaned.

"We've got to get the goods on them," continued Lindsay. "Inside information. That's the solution. But you can't get inside information from the outside."

"Oh, that's brilliant," I said, "absolutely brilliant!"

"There's only one way to go," said Lindsay. "*Infiltration!*"

"Infiltration?" intoned Heather.

"In-fil-tra-tion," echoed Ruth.

For a moment, I felt like I was in a grade-B spy movie.

"Right on," said Lindsay. "They're so smug! A little nosing around. A few clever questions asked to the right person at the right time, and they're bound to slip up. Then we turn them in to Mr. Kelly."

"But Ruth or I could never get inside the cool clique," said Heather. "We've put them down too many times for them to let us in now."

"You're right, there," said Lindsay, "but good old fuzzy-wuzzy Amy doesn't believe in making enemies with anyone."

"Now wait a minute," I said, not bothering to react to "fuzzy wuzzy." "You don't actually think . . ."

"Come on, Amy," said Lindsay, "you can do it. Rachael Harris already likes you. And what about Tony? He's on the soccer team with Mark and Davie. And you know how buddy-buddy teammates can get."

"But what does that have to do with me?" I said.

"Didn't you tell me Tony practically asked you for a date?" said Lindsay.

"Oh, Amy," cried Ruth, "you never told us about that!"

I shot Lindsay one of the dirtiest looks I could muster. When I told her about Tony, I specifically requested that she not tell anyone else. Now Ruth and Heather both knew, and they had found out in a way that made it seem as if I was keeping secrets from them. It was *so* embarrassing.

"You're way out of line, Lindsay," I told her straight, but she wouldn't let up.

"If you start hanging out with Tony, you could wheedle your way right into the inner ranks of the cool clique," said Lindsay.

"But I can't even talk to Tony without turning five shades of red and forgetting my name," I argued.

"You're not clinging to that old line about being shy," said Lindsay. "Look how great you did with reading *Sadako* and the talk show. You were fabulous!"

Lindsay took Marvin out of her hair and put him back in his cage. "After all," she said, "even Marvin bites sometimes."

"But this is different," I said. "You know how I am around boys. I just can't function. I can't breathe. I can't think. My brain turns to Jell-O; slippery, slimy, oozy, three-week-old rubbery Jell-O!"

"Okay," said Lindsay. "We'll just give up and let the club be canceled. We'll pretend we don't care about peace or justice or saving our own Mother Earth. We'll just sit down, watch television four hours a day, and be vegetables like everyone else!"

"Listen, Lindsay," I replied, "if you're trying to make me feel guilty, it's not working."

"Okay, forget about all that," said Lindsay. "Just

ask yourself this: What would Sadako do if she were in your place?"

"What does Sadako have to do with this?" I said.

"Just answer the question," said Lindsay.

"Sadako wasn't afraid of boys!" I said.

"No, Sadako wasn't a wimp!" said Lindsay. "I agree with you there. I strongly doubt she turned into a helpless mass of protoplasm every time a boy came within ten feet of her."

Now Lindsay was really getting me mad.

"I'm not a wimp!" I shouted.

"Yes, you are," said Lindsay. "You're a wimp of the worst kind. A girl who's afraid of boys. And you're going to stay that way for the rest of your life unless you face it once and for all!"

I was so mad at Lindsay. If she were standing on the edge of a cliff, I would have pushed her off.

"I don't care what you say, Lindsay Morgan," I shrieked. "I'm not going along with this hare-brained scheme of yours. Do you hear me? The answer is no! NO! NO! NO!"

21.
Yes

You know what a flight pattern is? It's the way airplanes fly in formation. Well, Lindsay and I have a fight pattern. We've followed this fight pattern since we were little kids. Usually it starts with some outrageous thing she wants me to do. Of course I refuse. She gets angry. I get angry. Then there's a fight, followed by a cooling-off period. Finally Lindsay apologizes (but not really). Then I feel guilty and give in.

It's a pathetic situation, I know. But that's just what happened with this fight. We fought about Lindsay's scheme to clear her name on Wednesday. By Friday I was putting it into action.

My first step was to get Tony on our side. Unfortunately, this involved talking to him. Twice I almost stopped Tony in the hall, but both times my courage failed me. Even when Tony said hello to me, I just smiled nervously. In my mind I said, "Hi Tony, good to see you," but no actual words passed my lips.

"You're worse than Marvin," I put myself down. "At least he squeaks."

I finally made the plunge in science class. Toward the end of the period, Tony volunteered to wash out some test tubes for Ms. Blum. I figured it was now or never. I could either sit at my desk and get a head start on my homework, or I could ask Tony if he wanted some help.

It was easy to make excuses: "It would be better to talk to him after school. No, I'll call him at home." But I knew I was only stalling. I got up and started walking toward the sink.

Tony was wearing a checkered shirt and brown pants. His hair was kind of ruffled and messed up in the back. Like lots of boys I've noticed, he only combs what he sees in the mirror.

"Hi, Tony," I said, stepping up to the sink.

So far, so good. Now what?

"Oh, hi." Tony looked up from the test tube he was scrubbing. Then he looked at me and wrinkled his eyebrows a little. I guess I must have had an odd expression on my face.

"Want a hand?" I asked.

"Thanks, but I'm almost done."

You should have noticed that he was almost done, you stupid idiot! Better say something, quick!

"Nice weather we're having," I said nonchalantly.

Tony looked out the window and smiled. It was totally gray and damp outside, the kind of day when all the clouds in the sky look tired.

Tony handed me one of the test tubes.

"You can wash this one," he said.

"Okay." I gratefully took the test tube.

He handed me a paper towel.

From then on, things got better.

"How did you do on last week's quiz?" he asked.

It was just a simple question. But somehow it made all the difference. I felt the tension ebb away like an angry wave sliding back into the sea.

Somehow my fear that Tony would put me down or make fun of me vanished. It didn't matter that he was a boy and I was a girl and we liked each other, because Tony was Tony. He was a person and I was a person and we could talk. I know it sounds silly to say all this. But for me, at that moment, it was a big revelation.

By the time the bell rang and we were walking out the door, I was able talk to Tony about Lindsay and the cool clique. At first it seemed like he didn't believe me at all.

"Mark and Davie have been nice to me," he said as we walked down the hall. "Maybe a little bossy at times, but, heck, they *are* the captains of the team."

"The trouble is, they want to be captains of the

whole sixth grade," I said, "and they want to score *all* the points."

"I still find that hard to believe," said Tony. Then he thought for a moment. "But I think you're probably right about Lindsay being innocent."

"She's innocent, all right. And we have a plan to prove it," I told him. "But we need your help."

"What kind of help?" he asked.

"Well, for starters," I said, "you have to help me get chummy with the cool clique."

"The cool clique?" said Tony.

"You know, the gang: Mark, Davie, Marlo, Rachael," I explained.

"No problem," said Tony with a smile. "When do you want to start?"

"The sooner the better," I said.

"Okay," he agreed, "why not start now? You can come down to the cafeteria with me and we can have lunch together."

I hadn't expected things to move so fast.

"Ah . . . er. Okay," I said, and we went down to the lunchroom together.

I had brought my own lunch to school that day, but when Tony asked me if I wanted to stop at my locker and pick it up, I said, "No, I think I'll buy lunch today." I knew it was a dumb thing to do, especially since I hate the food they serve in the cafeteria, but

I felt self-conscious about unpacking a homemade lunch in front of the kids Tony eats with.

So I went through the hot lunch line with Tony, picked up my singed chili dog and baked macaroni, and followed him to his table.

The cool clique claimed an entire corner of the cafeteria: four whole tables. Tony sat with some fringe members of the cool clique, two teammates from the soccer team — Roy Anderson and Alan Baker — and another kid called Lenny, whose last name I didn't know.

"This table's reserved," said Roy when I set down my tray.

Roy was so unfriendly, I didn't know how to react. I just stared at him with a stupid grin on my face. I thought Tony was standing right beside me, but he had gone back to the lunch line to get a straw.

"You lost or something?" snickered Alan.

Feeling the blood rush to my face, I almost picked up my tray and left. Then Tony reappeared with his straw. "She's with me," he said, and both Roy and Alan's hard looks softened to mild acceptance.

It was so odd to sit at Tony's table and see Ruth and Heather on the other side of the cafeteria. I'm so used to sitting with them. It almost felt as if I had become someone else. "That's how I should think of this," I said to myself. "Like I'm portraying a character in a play." Of course Ruth and Heather knew what I was up to. They didn't come over and say anything to me. They didn't even look look my way. I was supposed to be on the outs with them. That was part of Lindsay's plan.

I don't think Roy and Alan felt very comfortable with my presence. Most of the time they ignored me and talked sports with Lenny. Twice they tried to draw Tony into their conversation, but he seemed more interested in talking with me.

"Do you still want to make a tape of that Country Joe and the Fish album?" he asked.

"That would be nice," I said, taking a sip of luke-warm cafeteria milk. "Actually, Lindsay's birthday came and went, but I still think she'd like the tape."

"Well, I can't do it today," said Tony. "I've got soccer practice."

"That's okay," I said.

Suddenly there was a lull in the conversation.

"How do you like being on the soccer team?" I asked, just to fill the void.

"It's great," he answered. "That's why I don't understand how you can be so down on Mark and Davie. They're really good co-captains, you know. Everyone on the team likes them. Except for the kids *they* don't like. They get picked on."

"I'm not surprised," I said.

"I saw one kid get his glasses stepped on," said Tony. "Just because he has a funny last name."

"Leon Sportsnicker?" I asked.

"You know him?" said Tony.

"Just by name."

"It isn't easy to be a full-fledged member of the gang," said Tony. "If you're a boy and you don't have a 'girlfriend,' you don't really count."

"You really know quite a bit about this," I said.

Toward the end of lunch period, Rachael Harris and Davie Kroll stopped by Tony's table on their way to return their empty trays to the kitchen.

"Hi, Amykins," said Rachael. "What a surprise! How come you're not sitting with your Save the Earth buddies?"

There was more than a twinge of spite in Rachael's voice.

"I don't hang out with losers anymore," I replied.

Davie just smiled.

"What about Turbo Tongue?" said Rachael. "I thought you and she were best friends?"

Apparently the nickname Turbo Tongue had stuck to Lindsay.

"Turbo Tongue's worse than a loser," I said. "She's a lost cause."

Neither Davie nor Rachael smiled or reacted to that statement, but I could sense its effect on them. Of all the things I could have said, it had the most impact. A direct hit.

"Amy's coming with me tonight to Video Village," said Tony.

I almost said "I am?" but I stopped myself just in time.

"Way to go," said Davie, and he gave Tony a wink and a thumbs-up sign, as if he had just moved up a rung on the invisible but ever-so-real ladder of coolness.

22.
Video Village

Video Village used to be a luncheonette called Bakers'. The thing I remember most about Bakers' was its smell: a mixture of Mrs. Baker's perfume, Mr. Baker's cigars, old newspapers, and vanilla syrup. Bakers' was too run down to be much of a hangout, but Lindsay and I used to go there a lot. The pace was slow at Bakers'. It could take a long time to get waited on, and even longer before your order actually arrived. But they never rushed you out to make room for another customer. Lindsay and I could nurse a single cherry Coke all afternoon at Bakers'. Sometimes, depending on her mood, Mrs. Baker would give you an extra scoop of ice cream in your ice-cream soda.

After Mr. Baker died, Bakers' was vacant for almost a year. Then someone renovated it into Video Village. I had walked past Video Village lots of times, but never felt the desire to go in. As I followed Tony through the door, I knew why. It gave me such a creepy feeling.

166

Right where Mr. Baker used to stand by the candy counter, puffing on his cigar, was a pinball machine.

A Skee-ball machine occupied the spot where Lindsay and I always sat. It was like Bakers' had never existed. The only thing I recognized from the old place was the large curved mirror that used to hang behind the fountain where Mrs. Baker made our ice-cream sodas. The mirror still occupied the same spot on the wall, but its frame was now painted in a disgusting shade of Day-Glo chartreuse. Instead of good old Mrs. Baker, it reflected row upon row of blinking, beeping video machines.

When Tony purchased some game tokens, the man in the cashier's booth greeted him by name.

"Your friends have been here for a while," he said.

"Hey, Tony! Over here!" Davie waved to us.

"How are you doing?" asked Tony as he handed me a few tokens.

"I'm fine," I answered. It was sort of true. At least, I wasn't thinking about my *problem*. I just wanted to play my part well. If the cool clique had framed Lindsay, I wanted to do my best to get to the truth, clear her name, and save our club. Nothing else seemed to matter.

Marlo and Mark were playing a video game called Smash! There were two Godzilla-like creatures on the screen, rampaging through a city street. The object of the game was to smash as much of the city as you could. The one whose Godzilla destroyed the most, won.

"Hi, Amykins," said Marlo. "I hear you're not saving the earth anymore." Members of the cool clique automatically picked up on whatever nickname Rachael happened to give anybody.

Before I could respond, Rachael said, "Don't pick on Amykins. She's going to join the drama club. Aren't you, Amy?"

"I'm thinking about it," I said, trying to be honest without actually telling the truth. But something in my voice or manner must have betrayed the distaste I felt toward Rachael. I could see it in her eyes and the way she drew back from me.

By now Tony had picked out a video machine and was feeding coins into it.

"Drat!" Davie slammed the machine he was playing with the heel of his right hand. "I finally get to level four and what happens? I let the first Alien Zombie I run into chop me in half."

"Let me try that one," said Rachael. "It looks easy."

While Rachael took over Davie's machine, Davie walked over to Tony. "Step aside, pal," he said.

"Sure thing," said Tony and he let Davie take over his game.

"He's going to pay you for that, isn't he?" I whispered to Tony, who was already feeding coins into another machine.

"He never does," said Tony. "Later, if we're lucky, they'll let us buy them a pizza. You brought some money like I told you to, didn't you?"

"What!" I said, raising my voice. "If we're lucky *they'll let us buy them* a pizza! You must be crazy!"

"Relax," said Tony. "Don't you have the money?"

"Yeah, I have the money!" I said, shouting now. It took me half an hour to shake that many coins out of Piggy. "But that's not the point! Why should we buy *them* a pizza!" I was really losing it now. *"Who do they think they are, anyway?!"*

"Shhh . . ." Tony actually tried to put his hand over my mouth to shut me up. But it was too late.

"Hey, what's going on?" said Davie. "I thought you said Amy was cool."

Rachael looked at me as if I were a crushed bug on the pavement.

Apparently buying a pizza was the final initiation rite for becoming an official member of the cool clique. And I was being *uncool*.

Mark whispered something to Tony, and the entire cool clique picked up and moved to a different part of Video Village.

"Now you've done it," said Tony. "Come on, we'd better get out of here." He grabbed me by the arm and yanked me out the door.

The chilly night air made me aware of how warm my face felt. Although I had no mirror to look in, I knew it was probably bright red.

"What did Mark say to you?" I asked as we started down the street.

"He told me to dump you and come back later," said Tony, his voice cold as Arctic ice.

"Is that what you're going to do?" I asked.

"I'm thinking about it," answered Tony. His voice was colder than ice now, perhaps the temperature of liquid oxygen.

"You really care a lot about being a member of the cool clique. Don't you?" I said.

"Doesn't everyone who's anyone?" answered Tony, the chill in his voice approaching absolute zero.

"I don't."

"I rest my case," said Tony.

Suddenly I didn't want to be with Tony anymore. I wished I had never met him.

"Then go back!" I said. "I'll get home by myself!"

"You don't know anything about anything," said Tony, still walking by my side. "Mark and Davie have been good to me!"

"You've gotta be kidding!" I said. "They were treating you like some kind of termite back there. I don't see how you could stand it. I certainly couldn't."

"You should be thankful I took you here tonight," said Tony. "Your friends are weird."

"My friends treat me with with respect!" I insisted.

By now we were several blocks from Video Village, standing on the corner next to Hal's used-car lot. Except for a few cars passing by, the street was empty. Suddenly Tony sat down on the bumper of a used station wagon. His arms fell into his lap like two sticks of wood. With his chin resting on his chest, he looked like a puppet whose puppeteer had let go of its strings.

"You . . . just . . . don't . . . understand," said Tony, pronouncing each word separately as if I were a moron or a little baby who needed to have her food cut up in little bite-sized pieces.

"What . . . don't . . . I . . . understand . . . Tony?" I responded, mocking his manner of speech.

"It was me," he replied. "I was the one who wrote on the front door of the school."

I couldn't believe it.

"Mr. Davis is a warmonger! You?" I sputtered.

"I know it was a dumb thing to do," said Tony, "but I knew how much the gang wanted to get back at Lindsay. . . ."

Gradually it began to sink in.

"So Mark and Davie put you up to it?" I said.

"No," he said slowly, "the whole thing was my idea. I even called Mr. Kelly's office and told him I had seen Lindsay do it. I never dreamed she would get in so much trouble. Really I didn't."

Tony's voice had softened to a kind of pleading. But

I was just starting to get angry. What nerve he had! The more I thought about it, the more my anger bubbled up inside of me.

"So I guess you and the cool clique had a big laugh at our expense!" I said.

"I never told them," said Tony. "After Lindsay got suspended, even Mark and Davie were talking about what a raw deal she got from Mr. Kelly. I realized too late that underneath it all, even Marlo and Rachael admire Lindsay and what your club was doing. I was afraid to take credit for what I had done. Afraid they might turn me in. You're the first one I've told."

"I could never do what you did," I said. "Never!"

"Of course not," bristled Tony. "You *belong* here."

"And just what does that mean?" I snapped.

"You've lived in this town all your life, haven't you?" said Tony.

"So what if I have?"

"You don't know what it's like to be the new kid. Sometimes they make fun of you for no reason at all. They call you names and pick fights with you. You never have any real friends!"

It was hard not to feel sorry for Tony. But I couldn't forget what he had done to Lindsay. "That's still no excuse," I said.

For a long time, Tony was quiet. Then he wiped the back of his hand against his cheek. Perhaps there was a tear there. I couldn't say for sure.

172

"You going to tell on me?" he asked, raising his head to look at my face.

Tony's eyes were clouded over like the eyes of the little red squirrel that fell out of Derrick's fort. One searching look from those eyes and whatever anger I still felt toward Tony dissolved like a single teaspoon of sugar in a large pitcher of lemonade.

"No," I answered, "but you're going to Mr. Kelly's office and confess."

"I am?" said Tony.

"Yes, you are," I said. "And when it's all over, you're going to have a real friend. Someone who cares."

"I am?"

"That's right," I said.

"And who's that going to be?" asked Tony.

"Me," I said. "I'll be your friend."

23.
The Ultra-Grooviest

"Oh, Amy!" cried Lindsay when I told her the news. "I knew I could count on you! You're the best friend a person ever had!"

In a flash she was on the phone to Ruth and Heather.

"I've got this utterly cosmic news," she said, cradling the phone under her chin while opening a can of chicken noodle soup over the kitchen counter. "You've got to come over and celebrate! Amy caught the culprit. And it wasn't even someone on my list of suspects. Isn't that cosmic?"

Plop! The soup slid out of the can across the counter and onto the floor.

"Good!" cried Lindsay. "Who wants to eat soup at a cosmic time like this? This calls for celebration food! This calls for pizza!"

"You've changed your favorite word," I commented.

"Yeah, 'dynamic' wasn't cosmic enough," said Lindsay, reaching into her jeans. "Remember these?" From her pocket she pulled the free Pizza Boy pizza coupons.

174

"I think now would be a good time to cash these in. Don't you agree?"

The Pizza Boy pizza lady who took our order over the phone was very nice. When Lindsay told her how we had won the free coupons in a talent contest, she threw in extra cheese, mushrooms, pepperoni, peppers, onions, and olives, for no extra charge.

Ruth and Heather arrived, screeching and squealing.

"This is the ultra-grooviest!" gushed Ruth, bursting through the door.

"The super-ultra-grooviest with a cherry on top!" cried Heather, and all four of us did the peace handshake.

We were making so much noise, Lindsay's mom, who was working in the den on her word processor, had to holler at us to quiet down.

While we waited for the pizza to be delivered, Ruth and Heather had me repeat the story of Tony's confession at least three times.

"So he did it to be accepted into the cool clique," said Heather. "Who would have guessed?"

When the pizza arrived, Lindsay took a slice to her mother. I think it was then that she told her about Tony's confession. I couldn't hear what they were saying, but I saw Lindsay's mom stand up and give Lindsay a hug.

They didn't talk long. When Lindsay came back,

all she said was, "Carol has another deadline."

"There's something about Saturday and pizza that goes together," said Ruth. "Don't you agree?"

"Yeah," said Heather, "like movies and popcorn."

"Like carnivals and cotton candy," said Lindsay.

"Like hot chocolate and marshmallows!"

"Ooooo! What a good idea!" said Ruth, turning to Lindsay. "You got any?"

She did, and we mixed up a batch. While it simmered on the stove, we finished the last slice of pizza, scraping what remained of the cheese that was stuck to the lid of the cardboard box.

"And look what I found," said Lindsay. In her left hand was a bag of marshmallows; in her right, a jar of roasted peanuts.

"When did you find out it was Tony?" asked Heather, popping a handful of peanuts into her mouth.

"Last night," I replied, taking the jar from her hand.

"Last night!" said Lindsay. "Why didn't you call me sooner?"

"It was late," I replied.

"Then you should have called me first thing this morning," said Lindsay.

"I was helping my mom clean the oven," I explained.

"Oh." Lindsay frowned disapprovingly.

"When is Tony going to tell Mr. Kelly?" asked Ruth.

"Monday," I replied, washing down a mouthful of roasted peanuts with a few sips of hot chocolate.

"What if he doesn't?" said Heather.

"Don't worry, he will," I reassured her.

"Sounds like you really trust him," said Ruth.

"Yes, as a matter of fact, I do trust him," I replied quite sincerely.

"Well, it doesn't matter," said Lindsay. "If he doesn't confess, we'll turn the bugger in!"

Just then, the phone rang.

"If it's for me, I'll ring them back later," Lindsay called to her mom.

"It's for Amy," said Mrs. Morgan.

"Is it my mom?" I asked.

"No, it's a young man," she replied.

Could it be Derrick? I wondered as I picked up the receiver.

"Hi," said a familiar voice, "this is Tony."

My first thought was that something was wrong.

"What is it? Are you in trouble?" I asked.

"No, should I be?" replied Tony with a smile in his voice. "I was wondering if maybe you'd like to go to a movie with me this afternoon?"

Suddenly I became very aware of the fact that Lindsay and the twins were staring at me. Going to the movies with Tony sounded great, but how could I say yes with them standing right there?

"Who is it?" whispered Lindsay.

"It's Tony!" I said, holding my hand over the receiver.

"If he's trying to take back his confession, tell him it's too late," said Lindsay.

I turned back to the phone. "Gosh, I'm kind of busy this afternoon."

"Oh, I see," said Tony and I heard the smile in his voice shrivel up like month-old roses.

"The nerve of that kid. Calling *my* house!" grumbled Lindsay. "Tell him to get lost! Hang up on him!"

Suddenly I became very annoyed. But not with Tony. "When is the movie?" I asked.

"It starts at two."

I glanced at Lindsay's kitchen clock. It was already one-thirty. "Okay," I said, "I'll go."

"You will?" he said, and I sensed Tony's smile beaming through the receiver again. "Shall I pick you up at Lindsay's?"

"No!" I said firmly, "I'll meet you there."

24.
The Date

Ruth and Heather thought it was "super-groovy" that I was going to a movie with Tony. But Lindsay pulled me out of the kitchen.

"You're not really going on a *date* with that creep, are you?" she said, holding the sleeve of my sweater.

"I most certainly am," I replied, wrenching my arm free. "And Tony's not a creep!"

"Oh, no?" said Lindsay. "He only got me suspended and nearly ruined our Save the Earth Club. What do you call that?" Lindsay's eyes pinned me to the wall.

"He didn't do it to hurt us," I said. "Besides, he confessed."

"Only because we flushed him out," said Lindsay.

"That's not true and you know it!" I shouted.

"All I know is that Tony Barlucci is *not* my friend. In fact, I've got every reason to believe he's my enemy. And if you go with him to the movies, *you're* not my friend, either!"

For a moment I just stared at Lindsay, astounded.

How could she say such a thing to *me*?

"You're making a big mistake, Lindsay!" I said and grabbed my things off the dining room table. "A really big mistake. A cosmic one, in fact!"

"And you're running away from the truth," said Lindsay, crossing her arms smugly.

"The truth is that you're about as grateful as a pine-cone!" I retorted.

Ruth and Heather had left the kitchen by this time and were standing in the hall looking like two frightened rabbits. I guess no one in their family ever had the kind of shouting match that Lindsay and I were having now.

"Come on, you guys," said Heather. "Make peace!"

"Yeah, let's try to work this out like adults," said Ruth.

"Like adults!" huffed Lindsay. "You want us to buy guns and shoot each other? That's how adults work out their problems!"

"Lindsay's just jealous, that's all," I said.

"Jealous? Ha!" Lindsay forced out a grotesque laugh.

"You can laugh all you want," I said, "but I'm not going to stick around here and listen to your abuse anymore. Tony's waiting."

"Yeah, well, I don't care where you go," said Lindsay, "because you're nothing but a dirty little traitor."

That was it! I grabbed my things and left.

"Traitor!" Lindsay called out the door after me.

I was so upset crossing Glenview Avenue, I almost walked into a moving garbage truck.

"Don't think about Lindsay," I muttered to myself as I stomped down the sidewalk. "Don't let her spoil your day. Think about Tony. Yeah, that's it! Think about Tony. And smile!" I forced myself to smile. But I couldn't put Lindsay out of my mind. She probably thought she would be the first of us to have a real date. She'd come back all a-flutter and tell me how cosmic it was. And I'd just sit there, wide-eyed, taking it all in. *Well, that's not how it's working out. Is it, Linds?*

"Excuse me?" said a woman standing next to me at the corner of Grant and Main Street.

I must have been talking out loud to myself.

"Sorry," I said and crossed against the light.

When I arrived at the cinema, Tony was waiting for me with tickets in hand.

"Want some popcorn?" he asked a little nervously.

Suddenly, Lindsay didn't seem so important anymore.

"No, thanks," I said. I like popcorn, but my stomach was still grumbling with all the stuff I had eaten at Lindsay's.

"Okay," said Tony, "I'll get large instead of jumbo. Have you seen part three?"

It dawned on me that I hadn't bothered to ask Tony what movie we were seeing. But one glance at the posters in the lobby and it wasn't hard to guess.

"You mean part three of *Mosquito Madness?*" I asked. "I haven't seen part one yet."

"Then you're going to love part four," said Tony. "I hear it's even better than the second one. Is it okay if we sit in the middle?"

"Sure," I replied.

"Good," said Tony and he proceeded to count out all the rows and seats in the theater to find the two seats that were in the *exact* middle.

"I like to sit *right* in the middle," explained Tony.

As soon as we were settled in, Tony started in on the popcorn.

"This is really good," he said. "Lots of butter. Sure you don't want some?"

"No, thanks," I said as my stomach gurgled with chocolate, pizza, peanuts, and marshmallows.

Mosquito Madness was about a mad scientist who loved insects and hated people. All of his experiments ended up as failures until he invented a secret formula that made mosquitoes grow to the size of collie dogs. Then the gory part started: giant mosquitoes crashing through windows and sucking the blood out of people's veins like vampires. The special effects were pretty gruesome, but apparently the couple necking two rows ahead of us didn't notice. In fact, *Mosquito Madness: Part IV* seemed to be having quite a romantic effect on them.

Right in the middle of someone getting the blood

sucked out of their stomach, Tony yawned and stretched his arms out above his head. He only brought one arm down to hold his popcorn. The other arm ended up on the back of my chair.

Mmmmm, what's happening? I wondered as Tony's arm slid down to my shoulder. I thought we might hold hands, but I hadn't expected this.

Out of sheer nervousness, I reached over and sampled some of Tony's popcorn.

As Tony's arm began to pull me closer, I shoveled the popcorn into my mouth as fast as I could swallow it.

Then the thought struck: I think he wants to kiss me!

Suddenly I pictured my mother sitting in the empty seat next to me. I sensed her leaning over and whispering in my ear, "You should be home studying. You'll never get into a good college this way!"

In the seat behind me, I pictured Lindsay leaning forward and whispering in my other ear, "Traitor!"

"Leave me alone! Both of you!" I mumbled.

"What? Am I bothering you?" asked Tony.

"No," I smiled, "it's fine."

Tony leaned closer. "Do you want to kiss?" he whispered.

My mouth was full of popcorn. So I just nodded my head.

Then I swallowed as we turned to look at one another. Out of the corner of my eye I saw a man chopping at a giant mosquito with a machete. Mosquito guts were flying everywhere! No wonder people always close their eyes when they kiss!

As our lips drew nearer, I felt something moving inside of me. True love? No. It was my stomach churning. Before I knew what was happening, a gigantic burp forced its way out of my mouth and resounded through the theater like a foghorn.

BUUUUUURP!

It was such a loud burp, the couple ahead of us stopped necking and turned around to see what was going on.

I don't think Tony could have looked more shocked if I had suddenly turned into a blood-sucking giant mosquito. For a moment I was afraid that he was going to say something mean or insulting.

Instead, he broke into a loud laugh. He laughed so hard, he knocked what remained of his popcorn onto the floor.

Then I started laughing. We both laughed so hard, we couldn't stop until the manager came over and threatened to throw us out.

25.
A Mystical Experience

We promised the manager to behave, but after he left, we looked at each other and cracked up all over again. It was even worse this time. Tony almost fell on the floor, and I laughed so much, I bumped my head on the seat in front of me. I knew it was rude, but I just couldn't help myself. This time, when the manager came over, he handed us our refunds.

"Sorry," he said, "you'll have to leave."

Just like that. No second chance. .

"That movie wasn't so hot anyway," said Tony when we were on the street again. "You okay?"

"Actually, I'm feeling a little sick to my stomach," I said, running down the list of all the food I had eaten in the last hour or so.

"You're lucky you only burped and didn't throw up," said Tony.

Although we were already a block from the theater, neither of us had said anything about where we were headed.

185

"Are we going somewhere?" I asked.

"I thought I was walking you home," replied Tony.

"Oh," I said and did an about-face, "I live this way."

"I threw up in my father's hat one time," said Tony. "It was right in the middle of a crowded church service. It was either in my dad's hat or on someone's Easter bonnet."

"How old were you?" I asked.

"Just seven or eight. That was when we were living in Kingsville, Texas.

"Look!" Tony pointed out a robin redbreast. "That's the first one I've seen this season."

"Do you think you're going to stay in Westfield?" I asked.

"That's what my dad says," replied Tony, "but he's said that before."

"I hope you do," I said.

It was so easy to be with Tony. Not only could we talk about anything, but we could be quiet, too. I never imagined that I could be that comfortable with a boy.

"Can I ask you for a favor?" said Tony when we reached my door.

For a moment I thought he wanted to kiss me again.

"Sure," I said.

"I was wondering if maybe when I go to see Mr.

Kelly . . . I mean . . . well . . . maybe you could come with me."

"I'll go with you, Tony," I answered.

"You wouldn't have to go in with me. Just wait outside, okay?"

"I'll meet you in front of his office Monday morning before school starts," I said.

"Good," said Tony. "The sooner I get it over with, the better."

Then he leaned forward and kissed me just long enough for me to kiss him back. This time there was no burp, and the feeling I felt inside of me was not an upset stomach.

When Tony left, I was in absolute bliss. A haze of soft blue mist surrounded everything I saw. Happily I floated through the front door and headed upstairs to my room. I knew I was in an altered state of consciousness, but I didn't know how deep it went until I passed Derrick in the hall and felt nothing but utter love for him, even though he was carrying a shoe box full of chemicals that he had stolen from my old chemistry set.

"What are you doing with that stuff?" I asked.

"Making nerve gas," he replied. "Want to try some?"

What a creative child, I thought as I closed the door to my room.

No sooner had I collapsed onto my bed than the phone rang. It was Lindsay. I don't remember exactly what she said, but the gist of it was that she was willing to make up if I would forget about Tony.

I didn't even let her finish talking. I just quietly hung up the phone.

26.
Dust!

Neither Tony nor I wanted to become grist for the rumor mill at Lincoln School. So we kept our "friendship" quiet. On weekends we went to the movies and took long walks together. We often did our homework at one another's house. But we never held hands in school or did anything that would give anyone cause to accuse us of "going steady."

Tony went to Mr. Kelly's office and confessed, just as he said he would. Mr. Kelly let him off easy, with just a week's after-school detention. According to the twins, Lindsay was outraged when she heard about it. She claimed it was "a miscarriage of justice of cosmic proportions!"

"Why should I be suspended," she complained, "while the actual culprit is punished with mere detention!"

In my opinion, Mr. Kelly was more than fair with Lindsay. After all, she did call him a jerk right to his face. Mr. Kelly made an announcement over the PA system, clearing Lindsay's name of any connection with school vandalism. And of course he reinstated our Save the Earth Club. But Lindsay felt wronged and was not about to let Mr. Kelly, or me, for that matter, off the hook.

I felt sad about Lindsay's decision to disown me. But I wasn't about to give up Tony just to make her feel good. I had to draw the line somewhere.

It was like we had gotten a divorce. From that day on, Lindsay didn't call me on the phone and I didn't call her. We didn't visit during or after school. We didn't write notes to one another. We didn't say hello when we passed in the hall, or even look at one another if we could avoid it. As far as I was concerned, our friendship was ancient history — done, finished, dust!

Of course the twins refused to see it that way. In school or out of school, no matter what else was going on, they always managed to bring up what they called "the rift." It was so annoying, especially at lunchtime.

I remember one day in particular. I had just endured a really tough social studies test. My brain was feeling numb. All I wanted to do was sit in the cafeteria and eat my bologna sandwich in peace. I didn't care what we talked about. Even discussing the weather would have been fine with me. But Ruth and Heather had other plans. As soon as Ruth started complaining about her toddler cousins, I sensed my daily lecture lurking in the wings.

"It's such a drag baby-sitting for them. All they ever do is jab each other in the ribs. . . ." She rambled on and on, but I already knew where she was heading. "And you know who they remind me of?" she said at last.

"No, let me guess . . ." I answered. "Calvin and Hobbes? Peter Pan and Captain Hook? The werewolf and Frankenstein?"

"You and Lindsay," said Ruth. "That's who they remind me of!"

"That's right," said Heather in a motherly tone of voice. "You and Lindsay are just like itsy-bitsy little babies fighting over a toy. But babies don't stay angry at one another for so long. Even teeny-weeny babies have more sense than that!"

From past experience I knew there was no stopping them once they got going. So I just sat there, chewing on my bologna sandwich, waiting for them to finish.

"Disgusting!" said Heather, and Ruth did her one better delivering what was for her the ultimate put-down: "*Ungroovy!*"

One night, I got a call from the twins.

"We've got something to show you," said Ruth. "Can you come over?"

I had just finished helping with the dishes and I was planning on calling Tony before I attacked my homework, so I was not in the mood to go anywhere.

"What is it?" I asked.

"The whales are in," said Heather, talking on the extension line.

"Yes, our babies have arrived," beamed Ruth. "The envelope was waiting for us when we got home."

"It's about time," I said.

"You coming over?"

I hesitated, but only for a moment. "Okay, I'll be right over," I said. Then I stopped myself. "What about Lindsay?"

"Don't worry about Lindsay being here," said Ruth.

"Good," I replied, and went right over.

I was sure they wouldn't dare invite us both over at the same time. But when I walked into the twins' bedroom, there was Lindsay, standing by the window looking at the photos of our adopted whales! Judging from her expression, she was as surprised to see me as I was to see her.

"I thought you said Lindsay wasn't going to be here?" I whispered angrily to Ruth.

"I didn't say that," Ruth shot back. "I said don't *worry* about her being here."

I knew Ruth's and Heather's intentions were good. And I was touched by the fact that they had actually cleaned up their room for the occasion. They hadn't done that since the painters came two years ago.

"Oh, Amy, come look." Heather took me by the hand and dragged me over to the window. "Aren't they cute? Especially Salt. I think he's adorable."

Salt and Cat's Paw were the names of our adopted whales.

"Oh, no," disagreed Ruth. "I think Cat's Paw is so much sweeter. What do you think, Amy?"

All I could see of Salt and Cat's Paw were two fins sticking up out of the water like two pancake flippers protruding from a bowl of batter.

"They look more or less the same to me," I grumbled and backed away. Just being in the same room with Lindsay made my skin crawl.

"I've got to go now," said Lindsay.

"Why don't you two stay for some hot chocolate?" said Ruth. There was a note of desperation in her voice. "We can look over the information packet together."

"It'll be just like old times," said Heather.

I felt sorry for the twins. Their attempt to reconcile the divorced couple that Lindsay and I had become just wasn't working. As far as I was concerned, Lindsay could have custody of both whales.

"Lindsay can stay," I said. "I've got to go."

"No, you stay," said Lindsay. "I'll go."

Then, suddenly, Heather stomped her foot on the floor. "Can't you two do anything besides argue?" she exploded.

That night as I lay on my bed, I thought about what Heather had said. Downstairs, Mom and Dad were watching an Arnold Schwarzenegger movie. The sound of Hollywood gunfire mixed with Derrick's voice as he played with his toy soldiers in his room: *"Bam! Bam! Bam!* Die, you dirty raghead!"

There must be something terribly wrong with this world, I thought to myself. How can enemies be expected to make peace when even good friends can't get along?

It was too late in the evening to call Tony. So I shut my eyes and waited to fall asleep.

I saw myself sitting on a park bench at night. The trees around were green and lush. Not far from where I was sitting was a statue of a young girl. I'm in Japan, I thought to myself, and that must be Sadako's statue.

I stood up and walked over to the bronze likeness of Sadako.

How pretty she looks in the moonlight, I thought.

Suddenly, Sadako's eyelids blinked and the corroded bronze green of her dress flared bright red. I was no longer looking at a statue of Sadako. It was Sadako herself. With one deep breath, she came to life and stepped down off the pedestal.

"Amy, you look so sad," she said. "Tell me, what's wrong?"

"I must be dreaming," I said. "This isn't real."

"What you feel is what's real," said Sadako.

Her words made me feel both sad and small. I wanted to cry, but somehow didn't feel like I deserved to.

"There doesn't seem to be any point to anything

194

anymore," I confided in Sadako. "No matter how you look at it, my world is a mess. Even the good things seem meaningless." Then the tears began to flow. "Lindsay hates me! I hate myself!" I cried.

"My dear friend." Sadako reached out and gently held me in her arms. "Since we first met, you've grown a lot, and so has Lindsay. But friends don't always grow at the same rate or in the same way. It will take some time for things to come right. But trust me. Be patient. Stay true to what you believe in. Everything will work out."

I stopped crying. Sadako wiped a tear from my eye.

"But what do I believe in, Sadako?" I pleaded.

Everything seemed to hinge on the answer to that question. But Sadako only smiled and, stepping back on to the pedestal, slowly returned to bronze.

When I woke up, the house was quiet and, except for a full moon shining in the window, my room was dark.

27.
My Great Idea

Before "the rift," the Save the Earth Club meetings were fun. Now they were about as cheerful as a lump of clay. Before the rift, Lindsay and I had sat side by side. Now we sat at opposite ends of the table. If we spoke to one another, it was only because there was *business* to attend to.

After the talent show, our Save the Earth Club did a bulletin board project. Each of us took a save the earth issue and designed one whole bulletin board around it. My issue was garbage. I went to the library and did lots of research. Then I went through the school wastepaper baskets and pinned everything to the bulletin board outside the gym that should have been recycled.

Lindsay's bulletin board was about hunger. Ruth's dealt with the problem of water pollution, and Heather's focused on global warming. Almost every day at least one of us could find an article about our issue in the local papers and add it to our bulletin board.

This kept us going for quite a while. But Earth Day was soon approaching. Mr. Kelly was planning a school-wide celebration, but we still hadn't formulated a definite plan of how we were going to participate. I guess Ms. Peterson assumed that Lindsay would come up with an idea. But Lindsay wasn't cooperating.

One day at a meeting, Ms. Peterson looked directly at Lindsay and said, "Still no ideas? I'm truly surprised!"

It felt as if Lindsay wanted to make us squirm to the absolute limit before she honored us with the gift of her brilliance.

"How about you, Amy?" Ms. Peterson turned to me. "Any ideas?"

I couldn't believe Ms. Peterson was really asking me, what with Lindsay sitting right there. After all, Lindsay was our great idea machine. Why ask me?

At first, my mind was a complete blank, like when someone hands you a piece of white paper and says, "How do you like my drawing?"

"What drawing?" you say. "There's nothing there."

"Yes, there is," they reply. "Can't you see it?"

"See what?" you say.

"It's a rabbit in a snowstorm!"

Please don't judge my sense of humor by that joke.

But that's what it was like for me. All of a sudden, I remembered the dream I'd had the night I read *Sadako and the Thousand Paper Cranes*, and I saw the rabbit in the snowstorm.

"Ms. Peterson," I said, "maybe this year for Earth Day we could all hold hands around Lincoln School."

"I'm not sure I follow you, Amy," replied Ms. Peterson. "What 'we' are you referring to?"

"The students at Lincoln School," I said. "And the teachers, too, I guess."

"And what would be the purpose of holding hands around the school?" asked Ms. Peterson.

It seemed as if the only way to explain my idea was to tell Ms. Peterson my dream. So that's what I did.

"I can dig it!" said Ruth when I finished. "I can dig it" is hippie talk for *I like it*. "Holding hands around Lincoln School would be symbolic of holding hands around the earth."

"Yeah, very symbolic," said Heather. "Like what the hippies did in the sixties when they nominated a pig for president. I think the pig's name was Zippy."

"It wasn't the hippies," said Ms. Peterson. "It was the Yippies. And the pig's name was Pigasus."

"Hippies, Yippies, yuppies, puppies, what's the difference?" said Ruth.

"The difference was that the Yippies were serious about what they were doing," snapped Lindsay.

"I take it you don't like Amy's idea," said Ms. Peterson.

"It's weak," she said. "We need to do something more cosmic, like what the Buddhist monks did to protest the war in Vietnam."

"I don't believe Mr. Kelly would approve of any of his students burning themselves to death for Earth Day," said Ms. Peterson.

Whatever Lindsay said, I knew the real reason she didn't like my idea was that *she* hadn't thought of it. Although I was not about to say that, not in front of Ms. Peterson, at least, I *was* willing to stick up for my idea.

"If dreams aren't cosmic, what is?" I argued. "When James Irwin was a kid, he dreamed of walking on the moon, but everyone told him it was impossible."

"Who's James Irwin?" asked Lindsay.

"An astronaut who walked on the moon," I replied coolly. Boy! Did I enjoy knowing a fact that Lindsay didn't know, even if it was something that I had just learned in earth science class twenty minutes ago. "Ms. Blum said that everything that's important, from light-bulbs to airplanes, and even the theory of relativity, started with a dream."

The twins loved my idea.

"Sounds cosmic enough to me," said Ruth.

"Let's do it!" said Heather.

"I say we should think about this some more," said Lindsay.

"I'm sorry, but I've been stalling Mr. Kelly long enough. He needs to know what we're going to do for Earth Day by tomorrow morning so he can write it up in the schedule and have time to print it and send home a flyer," said Ms. Peterson.

The expression on Lindsay's face was truly pained. I doubt her creative powers had ever failed her so dramatically before. Without a better idea of her own, the only path left open to her was to take over my idea. That way, if it failed, she could say, "I told you so," and if it succeeded, she could take credit.

"It's a dumb idea, but let's say we go with holding hands around the school," said Lindsay. "Then I say not just anyone should be able to participate. They ought to have to do something to prove themselves first."

I don't know it if was Lindsay's tone of voice or what she said, but all of a sudden I lost control of my temper. "Prove themselves to who? *You?*" I snapped.

"They should have to plant a tree or do some volunteer work at the town recycling center to qualify." Lindsay pressed on as if I hadn't spoken at all.

"That's totally the opposite of what I had in mind," I protested. "The whole point of my idea is to find something *anyone* can do to show they care about saving the earth."

"Maybe it doesn't matter what you had in mind," said Lindsay. "After all, I'm the president of this club."

I was really shocked to hear Lindsay, of all people, say something like that.

"I seem to remember that you were the one who talked about us all being equal members, or have you forgotten that?" I reminded her.

"That was then, and this is now," said Lindsay. "As president, what I say goes!"

"Sorry, Lindsay," I said, standing up. "You're not going to get away with this."

"Oh, Amy, I'm so sick of your childish ways! Why don't you just quit if you don't like what we're doing?"

"Ladies, ladies, please, this will never do," said Ms. Peterson. "For some time now I've been watching you two, hoping that you'd come to your senses on your own." She sighed deeply. "A few weeks ago, you were best friends. Now look at you. Ready to scratch each other's eyes out! What happened?"

"They've been having a hate marathon," said Ruth. "That's what happened."

"We've tried talking some sense into them, but they just won't listen," said Heather.

It was so embarrassing to hear the twins talk about us that way.

"I finally realized what a creep Lindsay was," I said, attempting to defend myself. "That's what happened!"

"What a creep *I* was." Lindsay rolled her eyeballs. "*You're* the betrayer!"

"That's a dirty rotten lie." I turned to Ms. Peterson. "If anyone's been betrayed, it's me."

"Okay, okay," said Ms. Peterson. "Let's start from the beginning. . . ."

Just then, Mr. Applebaum, the school janitor, pushed open the door. "I don't like to rush you, ma'am, but I have to finish sweeping this room before I can go home," he said.

Ms. Peterson looked at her watch. "Oh my goodness, I had no idea it was so late."

"I think we should vote on this," I said.

Reluctantly Ms. Peterson agreed. "I did promise to give Mr. Kelly an answer by tomorrow," she said, "but I'd like to have a good long talk with both of you sometime soon."

Lindsay threw Ms. Peterson a hate look that could wilt a redwood.

"Okay," I said. "All those in favor of letting everyone participate, signify by saying 'Aye.' "

"Aye," said Ruth.

"Aye," said Heather.

"Aye . . ." Lindsay began.

"Good," said Ms. Peterson. "Then the matter is settled."

"I . . . quit!" said Lindsay, and she stomped out of the room.

28.
98.6

April twenty-second, Earth Day. I woke up feeling as if I'd been sleeping on a bed of rocks. My neck and shoulders ached. My throat felt like sandpaper. I heaved back the covers and stumbled out of bed. The sun was up, but it was still dark in my room. I turned on the light and looked at myself in the mirror. I look forty years old, I thought to myself. I felt my forehead. Oh, no! I have a fever!

I wanted to crawl into bed, pull the covers over my head, and stay there for about five years. In five years I'll be seventeen, I thought to myself. Things will look different to me then. Today will be a distant memory. The fact that it was my idea to hold hands around Lincoln School and I never showed up won't matter to anyone anymore. Even Ms. Peterson and the twins will have forgotten about it by then.

But I refused to let myself wimp out. I checked my tongue in the mirror. It was still pink. Good, I thought to myself. That will help fool Mom.

I went into the bathroom, took the thermometer from the medicine cabinet, and hid it in the bottom of my sock drawer. Then, aching and miserable, I climbed back into my bed and stared up at the ceiling.

I wanted to go back to sleep, but all I could do was lie there and think.

Since Lindsay had quit the club, things had gone from bad to worse. I still had Tony and the twins for support. But Lindsay had cut herself off completely.

Every time I saw her, she looked paler and more forlorn. Her curly hair was in tangles. She never wore blue jeans anymore, just black slacks, black shirts and blouses, black shoes, and black socks. She had even bought a black leather jacket to wear to school.

Lindsay not only cut herself off from her old friends, she shunned any new ones. Outside of arguing with teachers, she hardly talked to anyone. She ate by herself in the cafeteria. If someone sat down next to her, she moved away. She was absent from school a lot, often two or three days a week. Her grades dropped like lead weights.

Ms. Peterson tried repeatedly to talk with Lindsay. But no one could get through to her. Ms. Peterson even called Lindsay at home. But Lindsay would always hang up. Mr. Kelly sent Lindsay to the school guidance counselor and called her mother in twice for conferences. But nothing seemed to work.

Rinnnggg! My alarm went off.

I climbed out of bed feeling more tired than when I had gone to sleep the night before.

Mom doesn't always cook breakfast for us. Sometimes she doesn't even get up until I'm going out the front door. But this morning, as luck would have it, she was up bright and early.

"You don't look well," she said as soon as I sat down.

"I feel *fine*, Mom," I told her.

Mom took another sip of coffee and adjusted the sash of her bathrobe. "Grades are important, but I won't send you to school if you're not feeling well."

Ever since Lindsay's name had been cleared at school, both Mom and Dad had been a lot easier on me. I think they'd even come around to seeing the value of our Save the Earth Club. At least they didn't accuse me of being a drug addict anymore.

"Are you hungry?" asked Mom.

I wasn't hungry at all. In fact, my stomach was churning. But I knew Mom considered poor appetite a sign of illness.

"I'm starved," I said.

"Good," said Mom, "but you still don't look well. Let me take your temperature." She reached out and put her hand on my forehead, but I yanked it away.

"I'm okay, Mom, really!"

"Derrick!" Mom called upstairs. "Bring me down the thermometer."

Derrick, always a slow riser, was still getting dressed in his room.

"What do you need a thermometer for?" he asked. "Is somebody sick?"

"Just look in the medicine cabinet," said Mom.

"What is this? Some kind of dictatorship?" grumbled Derrick. "Don't I get to ask questions anymore?"

"Did you find it?" called Mom.

"No, it's not here," said Derrick. "Who's sick?"

"Your sister," said Mom and she went upstairs to look in the medicine cabinet herself.

Derrick, knocking his feet on each stair tread for maximum sound effect, came thundering downstairs.

"Whatever you have, I hope it isn't contagious." He hugged the wall as he circled around me on his way to the refrigerator. "You look like a zombie from *Night of the Living Dead*."

"Thanks for the compliment," I replied.

"Don't mention it." Derrick took some chocolate syrup and poured it over his corn flakes. "Isn't this a big day for you?" he asked.

"Kind of," I said.

"Mrs. Everett talked about it in class yesterday."

"Oh, really?" I said. "What did she say?"

"She said the kids at Lincoln School were going to all hold hands today," said Derrick. "She said it had something to do with peace and saving the earth."

"Derrick, have you been playing with the thermometer?" said my mother, returning to the kitchen.

"No, and I haven't eaten it, either," said Derrick.

"That's very strange," said Mom. "I've noticed that our thermometer has a way of disappearing at the most curious times. Good thing I bought another one."

Before I could say anything, Mom's new thermometer was stuck under my tongue.

"Well, I tried," I consoled myself. "Maybe if I'm lucky, it will be something serious and I won't have to go back to school till next fall."

While I sat in forced silence, Mom took away Derrick's cornflakes and chocolate syrup.

"Eggs, oatmeal, or French toast," she said. "Take your pick."

"But I made my own breakfast," said Derrick.

"Okay, eggs," she said.

"I won't eat them," he said. "Eggs have too much cholesterol."

"Okay, then, oatmeal."

"I won't eat that, either," he said. "Oatmeal makes your insides stick together."

While they were talking, I noticed that Derrick didn't have any of his war toys with him at the table. That was so out of character for him, I thought maybe he was coming down with whatever I had.

When Mom took the thermometer out of my mouth,

I asked him what had given him the courage to come to breakfast unarmed. "Aren't you afraid of a surprise attack?"

"It's Earth Day," said Derrick. "You don't play with guns on *Earth Day*."

"Oh, really? That's interesting," I said in a matter-of-fact tone of voice, while to myself I was thinking, will wonders never cease?

"98.6," said Mom.

"What! I don't have a fever?" I exclaimed.

"Look for yourself."

I snatched the thermometer away from my mother and read it three times. No matter how much I held it up to the light or turned it from side to side, it always read the same: 98.6.

29.
Earth Day Party

"Oh, Amy," squealed Ruth when I walked into Ms. Peterson's room. "WFSR is coming!"

WFSR is the local cable station.

"Our ceremony is going to be on tonight's news," said Heather. "Isn't that far-out!"

"The TV station called early this morning," said Ms. Peterson. "Someone must have told them about our plans. I don't know who. I guess it doesn't matter as long as we're all comfortable about being interviewed in front of TV cameras?" Ms. Peterson looked at me as she finished speaking.

"It's okay with me," I told her. What a difference from what I would have said just a few months ago!

"Too bad Lindsay can't be interviewed, too," said Ruth.

"I have some bad news." Ms. Peterson sighed painfully. "This probably isn't the best time to tell you this. But I'd rather that you heard it from me."

Now the twins looked distressed, too.

"Is it about Lindsay?" asked Heather.

"Yes," replied Ms. Peterson. "Her mother called me last night. Apparently Lindsay didn't go home after school yesterday."

"Lindsay wasn't in school yesterday!" I gasped.

"I know," said Ms. Peterson. "I told her mother to call the police. I think Lindsay's run away."

"*All those students participating in Earth Day ceremonies . . .*" Mr. Kelly's voice suddenly boomed over the P.A. system. "*. . . please report to the playground.*"

"I wish we had more time to talk about this," said Ms. Peterson, "but right now we have a job to do. After the ceremony we'll meet back here, okay?"

"Okay," said Ruth and Heather.

"Okay," I nodded, and we followed Ms. Peterson out the door and up the stairs to the playground.

As we went outside, the first thing I noticed was the blue panel truck, with the letters WFSR, parked sideways next to the school incinerator. A man with long hair, and a video camera perched on his shoulder, and a woman in a blue suit were standing next to the truck.

Ms. Peterson took us over to them and introduced us. The woman was nice, but very businesslike. As soon as the cameraman was ready, she brushed back her hair and started asking us questions like, "How did your group get started?" and, "How did you get the idea to hold hands around your school?"

At first, the interview took my mind off Lindsay, but only for a while. As it continued, my thoughts returned to my troubled friend. Where was she now? And why hadn't she come to me for help? Hadn't we always promised to tell each other our problems, even the big ones we couldn't tell anyone else? I knew it was stupid of me to think that way after all that had happened between us, but I just couldn't help myself.

Halfway through the interview, they opened the school doors and the students of Lincoln School came streaming out. First came the fourth grade, then the fifth and sixth. By the time our interview was over, the playground was full.

Then Mr. Kelly emerged from his office with a megaphone. The teachers had managed to keep their classes grouped together. But as Mr. Kelly herded everyone around the school, good friends in different classes drifted out of their assigned groups and started holding hands with one another.

Ms. Blum was there. So was Mr. Davis, and my English teacher, Mr. Klein. Mr. Applebaum, the janitor, in his gray work clothes, and the cafeteria workers came, too. The athletes and the apple polishers, the nerds and the cool clique, everyone was there to hold hands around the school.

"Okay, everyone, spread out! There's plenty of room . . . and watch out for the rhododendrons near the front step!" Mr. Kelly stomped around with his megaphone,

211

creating equal amounts of confusion and order.

"I guess we'd better join the others," said Ms. Peterson. She thanked the TV people and helped us find a place in the line that was now forming around the school.

As I took Ruth's and Heather's hands, Tony walked over to me.

"I heard about Lindsay!" he said. "Do you know where she is?"

"I have no idea," I said.

"I talked to Mark and Davie and about it. They're going to cancel soccer practice and organize a search party. You interested?"

"Of course, I am," I said.

"Over here!" Tony's homeroom teacher called to him from across the playground.

"Talk to you later," said Tony and he went back to be with his class.

It took Mr. Kelly about ten minutes to get the entire student body lined up.

It was impressive to see everyone gathering around the school, but all I could think about was Lindsay. I pictured her roaming the streets, looking through garbage cans for something to eat. She's always so drastic. What if she decided to hitchhike to California to see her father, and a maniac picked her up? Horrible pictures flashed before my eyes, and the thought that I might never see Lindsay again tormented me.

When at last we were all holding hands around Lincoln School, Mr. Kelly took some three-by-five index cards from his pocket and began to read from a speech that he'd prepared for the occasion:

"As you can see, the local television station has sent a crew to our school today," he said, his voice sounding very tinny through the cheap megaphone, *"because this is a very special day, and these are very special times that we are living in. You have learned in your history classes that even great nations come and go. But, today, for the first time ever, we face a crisis that has never occurred in the history of mankind before, the possibility that our very planet might someday cease to support life. . . ."*

Mr. Kelly's speech kind of caught me by surprise. I guess it was the first time I gave him credit for being concerned about anything beyond whether or not we run in the halls.

But Mr. Kelly never got to finish his speech.

Right in the middle of it, the school doors flung open. All eyes turned away from him to the huge, bluish sphere that now waddled out through the doors onto the school steps. The sphere, supported by two small feet, appeared to be made of papier-mâché. At least five feet in diameter, it was painted in many shades of blue, white, and green to resemble the earth as seen from outer space.

"What the . . ." Mr. Kelly's voice faltered through the megaphone.

"I am the cosmic spirit of Mother Earth," the sphere announced in an amplified voice that sounded like Darth Vader with a cold.

"All right!" I heard someone shout. "The earth came to our Earth Day party!"

"I've come with a message from the very core of my being," the eerie voice from the sphere continued. *"I come with words of wisdom from my mountains and my valleys, from my rivers and lakes, and from the depths of my oceans."*

Mother Earth jiggled a little as she stepped forward.

"I come with a message from all the plants in my jungles and forests and all the grasses on my plains, from all the birds that fly in my skies, and all the insects that crawl on my surface, and all the animals of which you are but one. . . ." Again, Mother Earth moved forward. *"Yes, that's right. Because I'm older and wiser than you, I've come with these important words . . ."* She was now standing only a foot or so from the flight of steps that led to the walk. *"Well, what I mean is . . . that is . . . what I have to say is . . ."*

It was becoming painfully clear that Mother Earth had either misplaced her notes, or was suffering from a serious lapse of memory. For a long while, she just stood there. . . .

"Well, tell us already, what is it?" called a voice from the crowd.

"What I want to say is . . ." The huge sphere waddled

forward again, lost its balance, and tumbled down the steps. . . .

". . . *Help!*" Mother Earth called out as she rolled toward the crowd.

Several of us, including the twins, rushed forward to stop the sphere from rolling. By the time we reached it, the tiny feet at the bottom of the sphere had tilted up toward the sky and fallen inside.

Peering into the hole, into the dark interior of Mother Earth, I saw two familiar eyes.

"I spoiled it all," wept Lindsay. "I thought it would all come to me. I thought I would have something cosmic to say, but I was wrong. I should have been standing with all of you. Instead, I tried to steal the spotlight. I *did* steal the spotlight. But I had nothing to say. Nothing at all."

"I thought you said a lot," I told her.

Lindsay wiped her eyes and looked up at me. "Amy, please, don't make fun of me. Not now."

"Linds, I'm not making fun of you," I assured her. "Your message was just one word, help, but doesn't that say it all? We all need help sometimes, even Mother Earth."

Then I reached into the papier-mâché Earth and offered Lindsay my hand.

Lindsay looked up at me, and a quiet peace passed between us. Though neither of us said anything, when Lindsay took my hand, I knew we were friends again.

215

But we weren't just the old friends we had been for so many years; we were new friends, too.

As Lindsay climbed out of the papier-mâché Earth, the cameraman from WFSR said, "That was great. We got it all on tape."

For a few seconds Mr. Kelly looked confused, but then he quickly regained his composure. "So you got it all on tape? That's good. Very good," he said, as if he knew all along what was going to happen.

Ms. Peterson pushed forward and gave Lindsay a hug. "So, it was you who called the TV station," she said. "I should have guessed. Do you realize what a scare you gave your mother?"

"I'm sorry," said Lindsay. "I'll call her right away."

"How did you build this thing?" asked Ruth, patting the somewhat crumpled papier-mâché Earth.

"I've been working for weeks on this in Mr. Applebaum's storage room," said Lindsay. "I used a big weather balloon for the armature, and Mr. Applebaum helped me build the voice synthesizer from old radio parts. And guess what? Next year he's going to help us build a float so we can have a Save the Earth Parade!"

"Us?" I said. "Does this mean you want to join the club again?"

"If you'll have me!" said Lindsay.

"Far-out!" cried Ruth.

"Just plain groovy!" giggled Heather, and we all did the peace handshake.

"Didn't you say there was going to be some music?" asked the woman reporter.

"That's right," said Ms. Peterson, and she gave the signal for someone to turn on the school's outdoor speakers. Pretty soon we were flooded with the sound of John Lennon singing "Give Peace a Chance." The sound quality of the school speakers wasn't much better than Mr. Kelly's megaphone. But everyone sang as once again we all joined hands around Lincoln School.

This time, everything felt right. I closed my eyes and let the blissfulness of it all seep in.

Though I couldn't see her, I felt Sadako's presence.

"Sadako? Are you there?" I whispered.

"Yes, Amy." I sensed a reply from someplace deep within me. "I'm right here."

At that moment, Lindsay squeezed my hand, and I squeezed back.